ELINOR
&
SHAKESPEARE

A Novel by
Gerald Sindell

The Knightsbridge Publishing Company

A subsidiary of ThoughtLeaders Intl., Napa CA 94558

For more information, contact Knightsbridge Publishing, 131 Towpath Dr, Napa, CA 94558

rights@knightsbridgepub.com

Printed in the United States of America

ISBN iBook: 978-1-56129-004-8

Table of Contents

One — The Cull

*T*his would be remembered as a step backward for civilization in London, the day in May, 1593 when hastily recruited ruffians, sponsored by Royal edict and incentivized per animal seized, roamed the streets, pounding on doors.

"In the name of Her Majesty the Queen, open up!"

The demand was echoed up and down the block as the search party swarmed the mews. A terrified middle-aged woman cracked open her door and the rough figure waiting outside firmly planted his foot in the jamb and began to press.

"We're here for your household animals. All cats and dogs to be produced."

Behind him a huge wagon slowly rolled along the street, full of howling and terrified dogs and cats.

"Why? Why do you want our little Bounder?"

The rough man pushed the door farther in and grasped the poor woman's arm in an unkindly manner. Her arms were trying to cradle a small dog. With barely a struggle, the man took the bewildered animal by the neck in a one-handed grip.

"You have heard of the Black Death, haven't you, Madam? It's these little bloodsuckers that are killing us all."

He produced a small slip of paper and tore it in two, handing one half to the woman.

"Your chit."

"Will I be able to come claim him?"

"Neither alive nor dead. 'Burn and bury' is our orders. Any other animals? Any cats? Don't hold back or there'll be a terrible fine to pay."

"No. No. That's all we have."

The man slammed the door shut and headed to the next. He folded his half of the paper and slipped it into his vest pocket.

"Ha'penny for me." Without breaking his stride, he flung Bounder into a waiting wagon. "And the end for li'l muffin here."

A small, older, bearded man with a trace of a stoop and almost dwarfed by his sheltering black hat took it all in, shaking his head from side to side in sadness and wonder. Avrahim Sneshell turned back to the cab that had just dropped him.

The driver pointed up the street. "Anyone you're looking for in London, you start asking there."

"St. Paul's is at the end of this street?" He gestured ahead.

The driver nodded. "I'd take you all the way, but you're better off walking the last bit. Sunday crowds won't let me through."

Avrahim walked up the mews, reached the corner and took in the sudden expanse. Before him loomed the fire-wrecked remains of St. Paul's Cathedral. Worship having long since moved outside, and this being Sunday morning, a crowd had gathered in the shadow of the cathedral for morning services. The preacher was making clear why the plague was ravaging their city.

"This death, this black terror, this is the actual hand of God, reaching down from his heaven and meant to smite the sinners amongst you."

His wild eyebrows almost hid his cold gray eyes as he surveyed the flock, seeing mortal sin everywhere.

"You!" A parishioner shrank from the accusing finger.

"Need you look any farther than your own dead? Have you not had your mother or father taken from you? And you! Yes, you! Has God not wrested from you a beloved? A daughter? Your only son? Who has not yet had the black curse at their doorstep?"

Almost no one looked up. They were all guilty, somehow.

"This is God's punishment for your evil ways."

His flock could barely hear him, as another crowd, not far distant, angrily heckled a small group of worshipers.

As Avrahim edged closer to the hecklers, he thought he could recognize a familiar cadence from the small congregation.

"…quitollis peccata mundi…"

Something in Italian?

"Agnus Dei, quitollis peccata mundi…"

Avrahim automatically translated the Latin to Italian, and then the Italian to English. 'Agnello di dio. Lamb of God.' Avrahim puzzled it out. "These people are holding on to the mass in Latin daring the spite of the protesters. I thought it had been gone here for more than thirty years."

He climbed some steps nearby to get a better view and to tune in to the Latin, enjoying its closeness to his own Italian.

Another commotion rippled through the throngs. A black horse had appeared and almost magically seemed to part the crowd as it approached. In a few moments, Avrahim could see that the horse was harnessed to a four-wheeled caisson helmed by a black-robed teamster. Restrained by the stakes around the bed of the wagon, six linen-shrouded forms rocked against each other. Walking alongside was a terrifying figure dressed in black and masked with a beaked face. The figure peered this way and that into the crowd. If the gaze held for a moment too long, that part of the crowd would being to pull away, as if the masked-one might pluck a man or woman from its midst and declare them dead.

The black horse plodded in Avrahim's direction, and the masked figure's gaze suddenly locked on Avrahim. The masked one ordered the driver to wait. Before Avrahim could attempt to flee, the mask strode up to him and spoke several words. For a moment Avrahim's expression turned from fear to shocked surprise, and then, as if nothing had happened, back to a blank gaze.

The masked figure pulled away and looked back once at Avrahim. He may have nodded back. It was impossible to be sure.

The caisson drew away with its terrible burden, the plague doctor following behind. The hecklers had lost their voice for the moment, and the benediction of the Latin mass rose up unmolested.

Avrahim left the square and soon found himself in a distinctly different neighborhood. Although it was the Lord's Day, in this little square shops and outdoor markets were busy. Families strolled, chatted and shopped. Children ran underfoot. This, surely, was the neighborhood where non-Christians had found each other. Since Jews were at the moment banned from England, these were certainly 'not-Jews'.

The not-Jews were enjoying their moments in the sun. Down an alley a puppet theatre violated the Sabbath with a raucous Punch and Judy show, enthralling a small gathering of not-Jewish children. The theatre gave them a respite from sorting out their confused identities. In the tiny theatre, life was simpler. Whap! from the rolling pin. Screams from the injured puppet. Laughter from the crowd. And a smile from Avrahim as he savored the thought of seeing his long-estranged daughter once again without her mask.

Two – The Observed and the Observer

Live rats by the dozen, in cages spread across tables and shelves, observed Dr. Elinor Sneshell as she deconstructed a particularly unlucky member of their company. Her notebook open to meticulous drawings and details of her progress, she deftly slit open the belly from urethral orifice all the way to the center of the lower jaw. A few more slices to create two neat envelope flap-like openings, some sand-filled leather pouches to hold the opening just so, and the rat was fully presented.

Dr. Elinor Sneshell was the singular product of a number of rich cross-currents in Western European intellectual life. Born in the northeast corner of France in the town of Valenciennes, tutored first by her father and subsequently by her grandfather, a physician who had fled the Spanish Inquisition, she was one of the few women in Europe with a profound understanding, and a passion for, scientific method. At fourteen she had been sent south to Montpellier, whose medical school combined the centuries-old Italian tradition of delegating thoracic surgery to the smaller hands of female physicians, with new influences and knowledge coming from Spain.

As she probed the rat's liver, looking for swelling or other signs of infection, she was suddenly interrupted by a rap at the door. She dropped her tools, wiped her hands on her apron, and eagerly opened the door. Avrahim stood there, a broad smile on his face. He took a moment to fix the mental picture of his daughter standing there, before crossing the threshold.

"The sight of a daughter's face makes the world Eden once again."

Elinor was touched by the tender words.

"Father."

She took his heavy coat and hung it on a peg near the door. On adjacent pegs were masks like the ones he had seen the black figure wear in St. Paul's Square.

Avrahim lifted up a mask and sniffed at it. "Camphor?"

Elinor nodded. "It is supposed to protect us, but I doubt that it is efficacious."

"From the Latin 'efficax' no doubt."

"Yes. Now English. Effective. But the camphor at least does keep people at a distance, so there's that."

"Even with the mask, I knew my daughter." His accent covered a lot of territory. Italian and French, surely, with a dusting of Yiddish.

"I was so excited to see you, I wanted to give you a warm embrace. Now we can."

Their hug was interrupted by the thrashing of rats. Elinor's father was bemused but not surprised by his daughter's surroundings. She had always been a scientist.

"You have friends."

"I am studying them."

He noticed how many of them stared at her. "It appears to be mutual!" Avrahim enjoyed his joke with a chuckle.

"You know that I am following the Death here. The rats are always nearby, and I think, somehow, they are part of what is attributed to the miasma."

"I thought the miasma is the fog that carries the Death."

"I don't think so. Not anymore. I have seen the plague come without fog. They say you can keep the miasma out of your pores by not bathing, but I have followed both bathed and the unbathed at the same time and in the same place, and I have seen that the filthiest people are the most likely to become ill."

"I worry that you are always too close. That you will become a victim."

From the very beginning of her studies in medicine Elinor had considered that she might eventually lose her life to some disease that leapt from a patient to herself. Eventually she had decided to not only accept the risk, but to focus on what the possible transmission modes might be.

"I should have already. I have been with families when the Death first arrives, and I have seen in large families, with two parents and a grandmother and five children, that within a few weeks, only one is left."

"We have all seen this. The tragedy is too much to bear for many."

"Indeed. But I am looking at the one who didn't die. There was something special about them. And I may have that some special protection, too. Or I would already be dead."

"May God protect you."

Elinor had made tea for her father, and they sat across from each other in the gathering twilight. Occasionally two rats would start a fight, but otherwise, the evening was calm.

Elinor watched her father, knowing why he had come, but not wanting to disagree with him. Or say no to him.

"I know why you have come to see me."

"You are an adult woman. What would I have to say to you?"

"That you're worried about me."

"I could say that. I am! But I haven't said that."

"You want to."

"I do not want to tell you what to do. I simply want to make sure you have thought about the danger of being here at this time. And to make sure you know you can come home to Valenciennes, to your people and your practice. And when this horrible time has passed over London, you can always return."

"When my Jacob died…"

Avrahim interjected, "A wonderful husband."

She nodded in agreement, barely pausing, "…the joy of caring for our little village together also went away. If I had never married, I would not have chosen to practice in a small town, no matter how lovely it turned out to be. I had always thought I would go to a great center of medicine, continue to study and refine my arts as a surgeon, and to teach other women."

"Each person must do what is right for them. We must make our own choices."

"I have. I do."

"Excuse me for seeming to pry, but does London not terrify you?"

"Disease, yes. London, no. I am in love with London. If the plague doesn't kill us all, then this is where I want to be."

Avrahim had a sudden realization. "London is a person, too. There is someone."

Elinor nodded. "There is a person. And it is not just about him, but also what he is creating."

Avrahim was immediately intrigued. "Is he a builder?"

Elinor tried to decide if that fit. "In a way, he is. The English presently are between gods, as you know."

"With the Romans being forced out? But that is more than thirty years ago."

"For one's beliefs, a few decades are a mere blink. The Roman church was England for more than a thousand years — the very warp and woof of every life, really of all existence. It was how you saw the meaning of the sun in the morning, how you saw your mate, your family, your village and your king. How they all fit together. When the Roman church was taken from them, it wasn't just their faith that was ripped away. It was much deeper than that. It was the very idea that there was faith at all that was weakened."

"The One Church was no longer."

"Indeed. And if the One Church could now be two, who was to say there might not be others that also could claim to be the One True Church."

"People are happy with their certainties." Avrahim was suddenly struck with a shocked concern.

"Are you about to tell me this man is a man of the church? Or a church? Maybe I shouldn't know."

Close as the two of them were, Elinor hesitated to tell her father the truth.

"He is a poet."

"A poet?" Avrahim wanted to make sure he understood. "Poeta?

"Yes. And actor. And he writes plays."

"How did you come to meet a British poet? Was he a patient?"

Elizabeth almost blushed. "No, no. What a thought! I only have female patients!"

"Of course. That the law here?"

"Certainly the custom. They are very harsh if they suspect one of broaching a rule."

Avrahim raised an eyebrow. "How harsh?"

Elizabeth hesitated. "The Queen's previous physician was suspected of a misdiagnosis. Also, he was Jewish, which added to the suspicions. He was hung, drawn and quartered."

Avrahim let that hang in the air, wondering if there was anything he could possibly say that she might actually listen to. Like a chess player imagining a wide range of options, he played them out. And then he gave up and retreated to his first topic.

"So how did you meet?"

"At the theatre. I loved his plays. But of course, I had never met him. And then, one day as I was going about my rounds, he and a friend of his approached me."

Elinor freshened her father's tea and told him more.

Three – The Caisson's Burden

I was inside my mask, following the wagon and our horse and driver as we gathered the dead. The wheels, as you saw, jounce with every rut, and the bodies do not rest easy on our journey.

Of course, when the mask is on, I have a kind of tunnel vision, so I nearly jumped out of my skin when I heard a voice right at my ear.

"Are you closing in on thirty this week, Doctor?"

And I didn't like the way he said 'Doctor,' as if insinuating I had something to do with these deaths. I started to speak in my normal voice, and then remembered everyone thought I was a man, and I preferred to keep it that way for my safety.

I peered around to see who was importuning me. I didn't recognize the one who had surprised me, but I knew the other to be Will Shakespeare, whom I had seen on stage not too long before.

"These two departed souls make twenty-two for the week, and we are but on Wednesday. I do understand your concern lest your playhouses be shut, ye men of the theatre."

Shakespeare nodded in agreement with me and retorted, quicksilver, "Soon to be men of the gutter, if you keep your tally."

What could I say? I explained that I had no choice. If we reached a certain point, London itself would fail as a city, and could even need to be abandoned.

The other gentleman, whom Will introduced as Kit, had gotten to my cart and was, to my great displeasure, poking at one of my corpses. He began to argue with me about the quality of my medical judgment.

"This is an old man," he declared. "Surely old age is the culprit here."

I could not discern whether he was making fun of me or not. I explained, "I am quite thorough. The hands were black."

And then Shakespeare piped up, and I knew he was jesting. "An issue of hygiene, no doubt."

And then there was no controlling them. They seemed intent on creating a little comedy on the horror of it all, right there on the spot. Kit nudged the other corpse. "This one was done in by his great appetite, judging by the evidence. Surely you can't confuse obesity with the black death in your count."

I was not amused. "She. That is a beautiful young woman you are disturbing."

Kit re-evaluated the corpse, and then sprang. "A pregnancy gone wrong!"

Shakespeare had his own thoughts. "A love affair with the wrong man."

Kit retorted, "Or right man, wrong woman."

"Whose jealous husband…" Shakespeare caught the thread.

"In a rage…"

I stopped them. "Did not give her the plague."

Kit appeared to accept reality. "Damn it all. Fate has put us on an collision course."

"I am afraid so. I'm sorry I cannot alter the facts. They are cruel at times."

I made a motion to my driver to get our entourage moving again, but Mr. Shakespeare suddenly had an inspiration.

"I trust your charges can make it to the graveyard without your further care?"

I acknowledged that they indeed could do so.

"Then come with us, Doctor! Will take but a moment and you'll have a once in a lifetime opportunity to witness the secret retreat of fallen gods."

"Are you trying to bribe me in some way?"

"Rest assured!" William was charming, and gave me a broad bow, sweeping his hat from his head.

"It won't work," I assured him. But he already knew that. He just wanted someone to join their adventure.

"I shouldn't, really."

But I did, Father. Hiding within my cloak and mask, I ran off with the theatre for a few hours.

Four — A Cache of Thrones

I followed Kit, and William, up and down mysterious streets, winding our way downriver along the Thames, where our great warehouses stand. At one of these behemoth structures, where I could make out the faded writing that declared the place had once been a butchery, the two men walked up to a door twice as high and at least five times as wide as myself and pounded on the knocker.

And then, in a most curious manner, a small door in the huge door suddenly opened, and a rather bizarre figure appeared, at first glance more an overgrown elf than man. Apparently expecting my friends, he motioned them inside, and I followed. The door closed behind me, and for a few moments, I thought I was in pitch darkness.

And then, as my eyes became accustomed, isn't it amazing how our eyes scale what they can see to the light available? Have you ever noticed the dilation of the eye, Father? It is most curious to dissect, there is so much less than one would expect. But I'm interrupting myself. Here is what I saw.

Imagine rows upon rows of carved wooden painted Jesuses, frozen in pain, affixed to their crosses, each hanging from massive iron hooks that had once held an animal carcass. And it suddenly struck me, I was in a charnel house of Roman churches.

After the king de-established the Roman rite, the churches were stripped. Stripped of statues of saints, which were removed and hidden away. Silver candlesticks and offering trays were taken to the smelter. Paintings, altar images, decorated ceilings were removed or plastered over or whitewashed. A thousand years of the expression of their love for their god, or gods, if you will, were devastated.

And now in the gloom I could make out altar triptychs standing on the bare earthen floor, masterpieces staring back at me, some lying in the dirt. The space was filled with statuary, ghosts of saints in all manner of poses.

The warehouseman elf bowed to my new friends and asked what their pleasure would be this day.

Kit replied, "We require a seat for a great man." As he said this he showed just how great the seat of that great man might be, and the warehouseman nodded, saying he indeed had many choices.

We wandered up and down the rows, passing what seemed like noble thrones of all kinds. Finally the warehouseman stopped at one that was particularly generous in width.

"Here sat a bishop," he told us. "Surely a great man."

William is something of a mime. And a gymnast. And a juggler, too, I think.

My father smiled at my enrapt thoughts of Will.

"A man of parts."

I suggested the British might call it a 'man of many parts.'

"That's the phrase I intended."

Well, he is. All this to say, that to test the throne, for it soon became clear they were looking for a throne for some play or other they were working on, William went through a whole deck of characters within a few moments, draping himself this way and that, standing on the seat to observe something in the far distance, crawling down to kiss the feet of an imagined sovereign, ordering the beheading of some wretch.

I was shaking with laughter inside my mask, and suddenly Will commanded me from his throne, "Doctor, I command you to remove your mask. You are among friends."

At first I took the command from the throne as carrying weight. But I regained myself. It was a pretend throne. He was a false king, at least at that moment.

I replied, "For your sake, I dare not."

He gave me a curious look, but gave up the quest for the moment. Instead he turned his thoughts back to the throne.

"Here sat a Bishop. When he formed his utterances sitting there, they conveyed certainty. For hundreds of years, and more, there were the heavens above, the Church in between, and the flock below."

Kit was listening, and he was also poking about the thrones. Finally he found one to his liking, and pushed and shoved it until it was close to Will's.

He continued Will's line of reasoning. "Then the late King Henry, in his glorious wisdom, gave us a new church. And he was somewhat perturbed when the people had the temerity to question whether Henry was, or was not, acting precisely as the Lord had instructed."

Kit suddenly became Henry himself, leapt to his feat, and surveyed all of England. It was quite impressive to do that in the dust of the warehouse.

"What is wrong with those filthy masses? So it's a different church, at least in name. And Rome no longer stands between the English throne and God himself. But your God is still the same God!"

Marlowe still seemed to be an angry king as he contemplated his ungrateful masses spread out before him. And then Will explained what was on their minds.

"And that is why, dear Doctor, we must bring one of these thrones to the theatre."

Kit added, "For if the people can no longer put their faith in the theatre of the church, they will need to find faith…"

And Will jumped in, "And laughter…"

"Indeed, in the benedictions of the theatre. Hence our joint efforts in a new play, in which the Devil chokes on

Faustus's black soul — I trust you have seen my Dr. Faustus, Doctor? — and spits him back to God."

"Yes, of course," I murmured, trying to catch up. "That was your play? Dr. Faustus?"

Kit appeared to be momentarily offended. "Does no one remember the author? Does everything think the actors make up their own speeches?"

"No, no, of course. I knew it was written by someone. I hadn't caught the name."

Suddenly he leapt from the throne and presented himself formally to me. "Allow me to introduce myself. You have before you the scrivener of the play Dr. Faustus. Christopher Marlowe. 'Kit' to my friends."

I took his hand for the briefest moment, fearing it would expose me. "Sneshell," is all I offered.

Will returned to the discussion of their new play. It was to continue the story of Dr. Faustus on a startling metaphysical journey. "So there is Faustus, whose soul the Devil once seemed to want so much, but now finds too evil for even himself. The Devil returns Faustus to the mercy of his maker. And the Lord, who is not pleased to have had Faustus thrown back to him after having rejected the Lord's grace, wants him not."

Kit was delighted at the dramatic possibilities of their construction. "There is Faustus, rejected by both the Devil and the Lord. Now he must make his own way both in this life and the next."

It struck me that this might seem like departure from Christian dogma, and there were courts to enforce such beliefs. "Will not the Court sniff a blasphemy here?"

Will didn't seem concerned. "None intended. And too well-obscured to be distinguished."

I didn't know why I felt such an immediate sense of foreboding. Even Marlowe's next words, although intended to assuage each and any of our fears, had the opposite effect. "I have kept our young friend's name off the page, to date. I can weather the tempest with my fame."

I spoke my own hopes out to both of them. "God, and Crown, willing."

Five — The Key with No Latch

Warmed by a smoky fire. Elinor waited and waited for her father to make the move she hoped he'd make. Finally, he opened his fingers that had remained tentatively holding his knight. She pounced, deftly advancing a pawn.

"Your bishop or your queen."

"Acchh. Can't I have that back? It was a mistake."

"You told me 'never even touch a piece unless you're going to move it.' You never gave me a second chance."

He was proud of her. "Maybe I was too hard on you. Look what a monster you've become."

That made her happy. "So. Bishop or queen?"

He made his painful choice, and Elizabeth collected his bishop.

"And this Shakespeare fellow?" her father wondered. "Tell me more."

"He is the most unusual person I have ever met."

Avrahim looked up, searching her face for a clue as to what that could mean.

"I'm not sure he's fully of this earth."

"Hmmm. Married?"

"Father!"

"You are among strangers. You can never, not for a second, forget that."

Elinor actually had no idea whether Shakespeare was married or not. She wondered why the question had never even crossed her mind.

Her father continued. "We don't have the luxury of trusting. We must always assume the worst. Assume we might need to gather our things and run. It is a hard lesson."

"I know. Spain."

"When my grandfather, your great-grandfather, respected physician to the monarchy, was forced to flee with his family from what had been our home for generations, he never understood. And never recovered."

"I really do know."

"And that is why I sent you to the nuns, to their medical school, so he could live in you."

"And I am grateful."

"And that is why you should consider returning to Valenciennes, where they need you."

"And that is why I am here. The nuns taught me to not just look for disease, but to look for cause. Not just to make treatments. Grandfather also believed there were causes to illnesses. Maybe too small to see, but there."

Avrahim shrugged. "I really did not think you might leave here. And possibly, I don't even think you should."

"Thank you."

With that, Avrahim stood up and paced about for a few moments. Finally he spoke.

"I have come here for a second reason"

He reached around his neck and removed a large iron key on a fine chain. He draped the chain over the key and held it out to her.

"This is the key to our home in Toledo."

"Oh!"

Elinor took the key and examined it. It was worn and heavy, for not only was it made of iron, but it carried the burden of many souls who had been dispersed.

Avrahim continued. "Who knows? Someday Spain may change, and we will be welcome once again. Maybe they will regret for what they have done and will give us back our homes."

Elinor puts the chain around her neck. "Someday indeed."

"So your friends. Did they write their play?"

"They invited me to one of their rehearsals. At Marlowe's theatre.

Six — The Pinch (Elinor's Story)

I sat in the shadows and watched a dozen actors in street dress run through a rehearsal of their work-in-progress. Marlowe spoke with the actor playing Faustus.

"Let us begin at the point where we depart from the old play, at the moment when Dr. Faustus has his final chance to save his soul."

The actor was confused, not really understanding when that moment might be. "Which text would that be, m'lord?"

Shakespeare jumped in. "Kit means where the third scholar says, 'Yes, Faustus, call on God.' And you say…"

Marlowe interrupted, stunned at Shakespeare's authority. "You know my play by heart?"

Shakespeare shrugged and patted his chest. "Where I keep all my treasures."

Faustus suddenly caught up. "And then I say something about God who I abjured and blasphemed. And then, ahhh…"

Shakespeare prompted him. "O, he stays…"

Faustus completed the line. "…stays my tongue! I would lift up my hands; but see, they hold them, they hold them!"

And then Shakespeare wheeled around and conducted the remaining actors as an ensemble. "Right. And the chorus says, in a single voice…"

All the actors, except for Faustus, said, "Who, Faustus?"

And then a curious thing happened. Marlowe held up his hand to stop the actors. They took him up on it, freezing their movements, holding their places. Shakespeare and Marlowe could walk around and through them, using the actors as props.

Marlowe took up the chorus's question. "Who was holding Faustus's hands? Of course, the answer is, the devil."

Shakespeare was excited. "And that's where we depart from your old Dr. Faustus! This is the moment when Faustus gets up on his hind legs."

Marlowe looked the tiniest bit hurt. "Was he not a man already?"

Shakespeare was too excited to be cautious about causing injury to Marlowe's feelings. He paced around Dr. Faustus. "He is last year's man. In the old play, Faustus visits the Pope."

Marlowe explained the obvious, "Who reported to God."

Shakespeare took on a conspiratorial air and stage whispered his observation. "But as we all know, now, the Pope is banned. At least in Some Places." Everyone knew he meant England. "So we have a new God at the moment, and he doesn't seem to need the Pope sitting on his knee, moving his mouth."

Many of the chorus gasped, sensing that what Shakespeare said crept right up to the edge of blasphemy.

Marlowe tried hard to keep up with Shakespeare's trail. "If we have a new God, then do we also have a new devil?"

"Yes. And a new man. Bear with me, Kit."

Shakespeare paced among the frozen chorus, looking at them all critically, as if there was something wrong with each of them. And the members of the chorus felt the heat of his disapproval.

"There is something about a chorus like this — the crowd that speaks as a single voice. They speak but I don't feel they…" he looked them over, "that you, are speaking to me."

Shakespeare was looking for the telling example. He tried one. "So when I say, Lucifer and Mephistopheles. Ah, gentlemen, I gave them my soul for my cunning,' you say…"

Hearing their cue, the chorus snapped to life. "God forbid!"

Shakespeare nodded and paced around them as they went back into their frozen mode. "Well done. But nevertheless, my dear Kit, when I walk around them, they are as silhouettes. They have no more depth than our draperies."

Shakespeare turned to Marlowe. "But when I walk around you…" and interrupted himself by reaching under Marlowe's doublet and pinching his butt.

"Damn!" Kit was unamused.

Shakespeare was gleeful with the reaction. "You see. A living person."

"And you, young Will, ought to have a living hiding!" Marlowe made as if to spank Shakespeare, but he danced gracefully away.

Marlowe was over his annoyance. "I still don't see it. I don't see the difference."

"Indulge me." Shakespeare said, and approached a member of the chorus. "Who are you?"

"John Waverly."

"Do you fear God?"

This was a personal question, which in normal company might not have received an answer. But Shakespeare was not easily to be denied.

Waverly considered his answer carefully. "Yes. On Sundays. Especially if I'm late to church."

The others laughed at this, but Shakespeare was writing a first draft of something. "And does he hear your prayers?"

Waverly demurred. "Not yet."

Shakespeare moved to the next chorus member. "And you. Do you believe in God?"

"Need to believe in something!"

"And the Devil?"

"Don't know what he believes in."

Shakespeare acknowledged the laughter and tipped his hat to the chorus member. "And you?" he asked a third.

"In fact, I am between beliefs at the moment."

Marlowe was confused, wondering where this was going. "And the point?"

"Maybe there is no chorus anymore. Just many voices, each unique."

Marlowe scoffed. "I think you are making too much of it. It's just a convention."

Remember, Marlowe was already successful and famous. Will was still getting his legs under him. But Will was struggling to make a theater of people who were more human, more alive. He was trying to make a better looking-glass. But he had not convinced Marlowe. Nor may he yet have convinced himself.,

"Perhaps. And yet…"

Seven — The Devil Comes Home

"Father, do you believe in free will? Do we have the ability to choose how we are to live?"

Avrahim silently sorted through a number of Talmudic stories on good and evil, but then he wondered why Elinor had asked the question in the first place.

"Are you asking this for yourself or a good friend?"

She was momentarily confused. "This isn't about me. I am asking for all humanity. Are people free to choose their path, or do outside forces, like Fate, control our lives?"

He wasn't sure how he felt, so he retreated with a joke. "That might best be saved for a deathbed question. Give me some time."

"When William was trying to get Marlowe to give up the idea of a chorus, of all humanity speaking with one voice, he was also trying to find out where the devil really was. For Marlowe, and for his dramas, the devil was a real person, busy providing temptation."

"It makes for a good story."

"It did. But Will didn't believe that evil was some outside thing. He looked at the devil and Dr. Faustus, and discovered that the devil was not some outside thing sitting on Faustus's shoulder. Instead, he saw that the dark voice was actually inside each of us."

Avrahim was not completely comfortable with this idea. "I have never heard that voice."

"Will believes it is always there in everyone, even a king."

Eight — Shakespeare Learns to Play

*T*hree tiers up in the Globe Theatre, Elinor had brought Avrahim to see Richard III. They peered down from their lofty perch as Elinor explained some of the odd aspects of how theatre worked in London.

"On the main floor are cheapest tickets — they call the people there 'the groundlings.' They tend to come and go as they please. Eat, drink, lose track of the story. Really, they can be something of a mob from time to time. If they aren't drawn in, they will start a ruckus. And they throw things."

"How often have you seen this play?" Avrahim asked.

"Thrice," said Elinor. "And as I told you, the new thing — the thing that provoked the argument with Marlowe—is that the central character has a dark voice inside him. He is—and this should not spoil the story for you—a murderer. A murderer and a seducer. A seducer of his victim's widow."

"And we are supposed to be entertained by this?"

"You will be. Richard Burbage will see to it."

As Elinor had predicted, the greatest actor of his day brought Gloucester the monster to life and made him human. Along with the rest of the audience, Elinor and

Avrahim gasped as Gloucester handed his bloody sword to the grieving widow, Lady Ann, giving her the opportunity to take her revenge on him for murdering her husband.

Gloucester seemed to be begging her, "Nay, do not pause; for I did kill King Henry."

She took the sword. Would she attack? If she had, the audience would have been with her all the way. But Gloucester wasn't finished. When she hesitated for a moment, he turned the tables on her. "But 'twas thy beauty that provoked me."

And now Gloucester took his sword and placed the point right at his own heart. If an audience member had at that moment leapt up on the stage, he would have had an easy time of doing justice. But as Lady Ann was frozen, so were the groundlings. Gloucester continued, pleading to be punished. "Nay, now dispatch; 'twas I that stabb'd young Edward," but then, again, flipping it, "But 'twas thy heavenly face that set me on."

Lady Ann let the sword fall to the ground. And that's when Gloucester pounced. He gave her the choice: "Take up the sword again, or take me."

The audience seemed to have stopped breathing. Lady Ann hesitated. Gloucester drew closer to her. Then he placed his armored hand on her fine ass.

Elinor glanced at her father, as if to ask if he was all right with this. He patted her arm, assuring he had seen far worse.

Burbage was particularly convincing here. The young boy playing Lady Ann was padded appropriately, lipsticked, wigged and rouged. Everyone knew that the pretty boy would be shaving in a year or so. But in that moment, letting the play work them, the groundlings were wide-eyed at the monster Burbage was playing, as well as the ghastly seduction with which they were now somehow complicit. After all, this was their own history, genuine English history, suddenly alive in front of them.

And also in front of them was Will Shakespeare, playing a king's armored guard, free to let his gaze range from Burbage to the audience, measuring how far one could go before the audience's desire to believe what they were seeing, their hunger to learn what an evil king might be capable of, would exceed their willingness to suspend their awareness that they were, after all, standing in a theatre.

So far he had found no limit.

Later in the performance, Burbage as Gloucester had become grey and wore the crown. Gloucester was now King Richard the Third. He confided with the audience, making them unwitting witnesses to his plotting.

"I must be married to my brother's daughter,

Or else my kingdom stands on brittle glass."

And then, as one might plan a pleasant outing in the countryside, "Murder her brothers, and then marry her!"

Any doubts? "Uncertain way of gain! But I am in so far in blood that sin will pluck on sin: Tear-falling pity dwells not in this eye."

A young sycophant to the king, James Tyrrel came on stage, shadowed by a page, played by Shakespeare.

Tyrrel gave quick bow. "James Tyrrel, and your most obedient servant."

King Richard drew near. "Art thou, indeed?"

"Prove me, my gracious sovereign."

The King seemed to be playing with Tyrrel. "Darest thou resolve to kill a friend of mine?"

Shakespeare watched the audience with concern.

Tyrrel was the perfect courtier, bland, willing to accept any command without even the slightest raise of an eyebrow.

"Ay, my lord; But I had rather kill two enemies."

The king was pleased. "Well, there thou hast it: two deep enemies, foes to my rest and my sweet sleep's disturbers are they that would have thee deal upon: Tyrrel, I mean those bastards in the Tower."

The audience was stunned: this was no joke the king was playing, and Tyrrel was the eager accomplice. Shakespeare was shocked at how far he could go and how much the audience would delightedly go along.

Shakespeare knew that his Richard III was a smash. He watched the final scene from the back of the theater after counting the day's receipts. The battle on stage was proceeding nicely, with lots of clanging swords and blood soaking through the costumes. Richard was in the middle of it, spun around and confused.

"A horse! a horse! My kingdom for a horse!"

Riding a fabulous white horse, the warrior Richmond stormed on stage, made a flying dismount, and without hesitation, fatally speared King Richard III through the neck.

Like a terrible clockwork marvel winding down, the clash of battle decelerated from a cacophony of metal on metal, to a few final blows, to the solemn finality of the clank of a helmet being dropped to the ground. And then, a welcome silence. Richmond held his bloody sword high.

"God and your arms be praised, victorious friends, the day is ours, the bloody dog is dead."

The audience was wild with applause, the actors took their bows one after the other, and then as an ensemble. From the audience, a calls of "Author, author!" rang out.

At the back, Shakespeare initially acted as if he had forgotten that he actually was the author of such an astonishing event. He was pushed and pounded as he made his way through the groundlings, and was given a hand to get up on stage.

For the playwright, this was a moment of triumph, the first success as he attempted to create a new kind of theatre based on a new kind of person. Richard was not written as a cork bobbing on a sea of Fate. Instead his author had given him choice, and insight into himself. He was evil because he had chosen to be evil. And surprisingly, it appeared that the audience was able to accept this new kind of person, and see themselves in him.

Shakespeare gazed out upon his audience, his miniature sea of humanity. At twenty-five he was marvelously young, and yet you could see in his eyes something unusual, a depth of understanding usually reserved for the very old.

And then it all came crashing to a halt.

Five officers suddenly appeared onstage, arranging themselves so as to create a barrier between audience and actors. An officer spoke.

"By proclamation of Her Royal Majesty, this and all unnecessary public gatherings are hereby prohibited, until further notice."

A second officer, seeing that the audience was momentarily frozen, thought it would be a good idea to add his own explanation. "Disperse! Disperse immediately, for God's sake!"

And with that, a moderate panic was set off among the crowd, and suddenly what could have been an orderly evacuation threatened to become pandemonium.

As Elinor led her father down the steep stairs, they were swept toward the exits. There was no way to go against the tide, and they allowed themselves to be carried along. Elinor wondered where Will must be at this moment and how he must feel.

Shakespeare was devastated. He took a long last look at his workshop at its moment of triumph and finality, sighed and exited.

Nine — Ink on Paper

The stately home that had come into fashion among the growing sixteenth century middle class had created a number of boons to industry. Top masons, leadworkers, and woodworkers were in high demand. Training household servants had become a new industry. The goods a stately home required, fine carpets, elaborate fireplace tools, grand paintings, each stimulated a new level of craft.

Which is where Richard Field's Printing Establishment came in. Lying on the backside of St. Paul's, where the shadows were deepest and the rent the least dear, the Field presses ran from before dawn and into the night, as the public appetite for books to fill the huge, new residential libraries was insatiable. The bookcases looked best when stocked with large sets of leatherbound complete works. Non-fiction sets were often sold by subscription, with order and payment being taken long before actual production.

In the hundred and fifty years since Gutenberg had created the notion of reusable type, the quality of presses and the men that operated them had continued to improve. Fields had divided the work into three distinct tasks: an inker who rolled the thick, greasy black stuff over the block of type that held the images of four pages, when eventually folded and cut, of a final book; the feeder who placed the large sheet of paper on the press bed; and finally the pressman, who turned the crank that pressed the inked block into the paper.

Although the bed where the ink met the paper was kept clean and neat, the ink had a tendency to get on everything and everyone else. Roll the ink on the block. Sneeze. Wipe your face. Turn the crank, but first wipe some excess ink off the side. Within a few hours the workers were as black as the fresh paper was white.

The feeder took a moment to wipe his face and hands with a rag soaked in spirits of turpentine. He blinked hard to get the turpentine fumes out of his eyes. Then, enjoying his fleetingly clean hands, he took up a freshly printed sheet, and being able to read, did so out loud.

"Here's something! What a lovely covering page. 'Venus and Adonis.'"

He scanned ahead and finally felt ready to make a public pronouncement. He was, in fact, delighted.

"This is filthy! Listen up." He help up the text, scanning with his finger. "'I'll smother thee with kisses;'"

The author himself arrived at the shop at that very moment. He froze at the sound of his own words and turned to watch the blackened trio.

The feeder continued on, "'And yet not cloy thy lips with loathed satiety, But rather famish them amid their plenty, Making them red and pale with fresh varee, vare-something. Ah!! Variety!"

The inker had never heard anything like this strange, poetic and, for him, pure pornography. "Famish them! I'm starving!"

The feeder enjoyed his audiences' excitement, and continued. "'With this she seizeth on…" He interrupted himself to puzzle over 'seizeth on.' "I wonder what he meant with that. I think he meant to say 'grab'. Or perhaps 'gropes'. He then took out a scrap of paper he kept in his pocket and scribbled a note.

"I'll fix it in the next edition, if there is one."

Field started to say something to Shakespeare, but Shakespeare was eager to hear the reaction to his poetry, and held up a shushing finger.

The feeder continued. "on his sweating palm, the precedent of pith and livelihood….' Whoa! 'Pith and livelihood!.' Boys, there's money in words of that high a pedigree."

But the pressman wasn't impressed. "Lot of good it'll do you if they throw you in jail for writing it."

Shakespeare tore himself away to speak with Field. Though eager and young and loving the theatre, Will was highly attuned to the fickle judgments of the Queen. She had often expressed her concern that the theatre contributed more license than wisdom to the common good. And, of course, the hovering threat of the black death made the future of the theatre uncertain. So in response to the threats from both crown and disease, Shakespeare had devised an alternate route to avoidance of penury: *Venus and Adonis*, printed by the older friend and townsman who had shown him the ways of literary London when he first arrived.

They clasped hands in friendship. "Townsman."

"Stratfordian!"

Field had news. "Are you aware that Marlowe has been warranted for some new manuscript that fell into the wrong hands?"

Shakespeare immediately grasped that the manuscript in question was the new Faustus and decided not to reveal his part in it. "Oh? A new play?"

"I haven't been told, but there's rumors of atheism. He's been up to the Privy Council twice, to be heard, fined or worse. But the Council itself has not seen fit to stand court for their own warrant."

"He must take caution from making more enemies."

Field nodded. "His temper is as quick as his wit."

"You know him well."

"I like the man, but I will no longer accept his trade."

"That is unfortunate."

"I must preserve my establishment." Field held out his hands, palms down, signaling that the Marlow topic was over. He allowed a smile to cross his face.

"And now to your Venus. The edition will soon be done, if I can keep my pressmen from constantly stopping and reading it! Very clever work, my friend. We should have finished volumes within the fortnight."

Shakespeare frowned. "I thought I had time to make one more correction of the galley."

"Obviously, you're too late. I promised you books in the stalls on time, and they will be."

"Fair enough. With the theatres shutting, the audiences will be seeking other entertainments."

Field let his gaze refer to his rollicking printers. "You may have hit your mark. Will you be waiting in London to see the response? Or will it be Stratford for you?"

Shakespeare shrugged. He hated leaving London, and he hated going away from something, in contrast to going toward. "Stratford is possible."

Field gave Shakespeare a warm, knowing smile. He had a feeling about this book. "Keep in touch. There could be revenue."

Shakespeare drifted over the to the press, partly to listen in, partly to watch his words come off the press, four pages up, sheet by sheet, fresh and uncut.

The feeder was reading while he worked, and his laughter was getting in the way of his work. "I'll be a park, and thou shalt be my deer…"

Shakespeare helped him out by finishing the sentence, "'Feed where thou wilt, on mountains or in dale: Gaze on my lips; and if those hills be dry…" Here Shakespeare arched a leering eyebrow, "'Stray lower, where the pleasant fountains lie.'"

One of the pressmen actually turned bright red, bright enough to even be visible under all that ink.

Ten — The End of the Story

In the shadow of St. Bartholomew's, Elinor waded through the cots that held the sick and the dying victims of the plague. Avrahim followed his daughter as she directed the nurses who attempted to keep order.

Having seen it all, seen months of unmitigated suffering, Elinor still had reserves of compassion, and was stern with her nurses if they failed to attend to each sufferer. The stages of the progress of the plague were all about, fever and boils, bodies turning black.

She pulled back a sheet to show her father an example. Large black blotches had transformed the patient into a Dalmatian. Particularly insulting was the disease's strange tendency to turn the nose into a black triangle, giving rise to the grim assessment of 'marked for death.'

Elinor gave the patient a comforting touch on the arm and brought his linens higher. "Ecchymosis. It resembles a bruise, but there has been no external trauma. If they are going to recover, the amount of ecchymosis attenuates. We have had patients stand up and walk out who are almost completely black."

She paused and turned to Avrahim. "Unfortunately, the story of my poet has come to an end. The theatres have been closed and everyone is disappearing."

"I am sorry. I know you thought a lot of him."

"I did. And he never knew who I was, except as the doctor rounding up the dead."

Avrahim again murmured, "I am sorry."

Elinor gave him a look. "You already said that. And I'm not so sure you meant it the second time."

But Avrahim did mean it. "I just want you to be happy."

"I'm not so sure about the importance of happiness. For now I need to go north of London. The plague is spreading, and I need to try to discover how that happens."

"By yourself?"

"Of course. That's how it is." She stopped for a moment, turned to him and touched his arm. "I will keep my apartments here, and you should stay if you want."

Avrahim thought about that for a moment, troubled by something. Elinor got it immediately. "The rats don't need to stay. I can have them taken elsewhere."

"Would it be valuable to your work to sustain them?"

Elinor nodded.

"Then I will become their faithful servant."

Eleven — The Widow Bull's Back Room

With the death of her husband, Richard Bull, a second-level bailiff and not much of a man for saving, the widow Bull had soon converted her large house into a public establishment that offered rooms for commercial travelers, as well as drinking and dining virtually around the clock.

Shakespeare stepped out of his cab and found his way inside. The widow greeted him while estimating the size of his wallet and any propensity for trouble.

"You are in need of victuals, my young man. You look a shade lean. A table in the grand salon?"

Shakespeare's eyes attempted to pierce the gloom. "I'm looking for a gentleman."

"We have but none else."

Shakespeare clarified. "Kit Marlowe. Christopher."

The widow nodded. "I believe he is still here. With several gentlemen. Would you be announced?"

"Not necessary."

She led and he followed through a large reception room, through another busy room, and then through a draped entrance to an antechamber, barely visible beyond.

Shakespeare nodded, sending her on her way, and drew the drape aside. He could distinguish three men, forming a triangle in the gloom. Marlowe, looked alarmingly casual, sprawled ostentatiously across a chair, his smoking jacket draped just so, a bowl of fruit on the table behind him. Alarmingly, because the two other men were anything but at ease. Ingram Frizer loomed over Marlowe, his coat drawn aside just enough to reveal the glint of his dagger handle at his waist. The other man was Nicholas Skeres, and he appeared to be Frizer's second, backing him up if necessary.

Shakespeare read the tension, looking for a signal, any signal from Marlowe, that would tell him what to expect. But Marlowe just took a plum from the bowl, and took a bite, letting the juice find its way down his chin.

Shakespeare broke the silence. "Kit?"

But Marlowe acted as if Shakespeare was a total stranger. "Sir?"

Shakespeare didn't get that Marlowe was trying to protect him. "Sir, indeed! And 'Your Lordship' as well, if you would."

"As you would. Your Lordship, kindly, these gentlemen have a prior business with me which must be attended."

Shakespeare had begun to read the situation and moved strategically nearer Marlowe, mirroring Skeres's distance from Frizer. He made his intention clear. "Mr. Marlowe is not without friends."

Frizer tried to brush Shakespeare away. "Take your leave, sir. I have business with Mr. Marlowe."

Shakespeare wasn't backing down. "As do I."

Frizer opened the fingers of one hand ever so slightly. In another world, the gesture would have meant nothing. But in London at the moment, with virtually every man armed with and ready to use a dagger, even the subtlest gradation of escalation was a language easily read.

Frizer kept his eyes on Marlowe. "Yours will have to wait."

Shakespeare loosened his coat, making it clear he was ready to leap if needed.

"I defer to Mr. Marlowe's preference."

In the midst of this crackling escalation, Marlowe appeared not to notice. "Mr. Frizer and Mr. Skeres were just leaving. We shall continue this, gentlemen, at some future point. My affair with you is complete."

But Frizer showed no intent of backing down. His voice descended a few notes. Everyone knew that when he hit the bottom of his range, there would be sharpened steel in the air.

"A spy is never free. You have taken our money while serving the crown, betraying both."

Marlowe was still the model of disengagement. "I have many masters, and dogs of low breeding are not amongst them. Now leave me, I have my meal to attend."

Frizer was enraged at the insult and drew his dagger, lunging toward Marlowe. "As you wish, traitor!"

Marlowe had overplayed his unruffled posture and was slow to defend himself. One hand went up to deflect Frizer while the other went searching for his own dagger. But Frizer was swift, and his dagger found a space between Marlowe's ribs.

Skeres stared at the wound for a moment, and fled.

Frizer started to pull his dagger from Marlowe's chest, but Shakespeare had already drawn. "Damn you!"

And with that, he ran his blade into Frizer's belly, stunning both of them. Frizer grabbed at the wound, saw the damage, and fainted away. Shakespeare glanced at him and assumed he was dead.

Shakespeare then turned to tend his friend. He knelt beside him and cradled his head. It was immediately obvious to Shakespeare that Marlowe was gone. He gently lay down his friend's head.

In the surreal moment, Shakespeare could feel everything slow down. The crowd outside the drapes was busy and loud; no one was coming in. Shakespeare felt that he was both in himself, heart still pounding, the terrible loss just beginning to flood through him, and at the same time outside himself, watching himself.

"There I am, smeared with the blood of Christopher Marlowe, my knife bloody from a man I don't even know, whom I may have murdered. William Shakespeare, what is this?"

And then he spoke to the room, and to the ages. "Here lies murdered the greatest wit in all of England. And to the murderers, a curse on your house — may no man remember your name."

But he felt more was needed. Words would transform the terrible and give this moment a chance at immortality. "And may the name of my friend, Christopher Marlowe, reverberate through the cathedral of the ages as England's greatest poet."

Twelve — Heading Somewhere

Shakespeare was packing, both hastily and carefully, by the light from a single candle. He tossed clothing into his trunk without much of a thought. But he treated his manuscripts with care. He wrapped the loose pages in an oversized sheet, and tied each packet up with twine, and deployed pen and ink to carefully identify each package. Some of the dramas, like *King Henry IV* and *A Comedie of Errors*, had already been produced. Others, like *King Arthur*, *A Knight's Tale*, and *A Roman Bacchanal* were destined to be forgotten, lost.

Mrs. Dawson, Shakespeare's landlady, filled the door frame. "We'll miss your presence, Mr. Shakespeare."

Shakespeare was momentarily startled. "Ah, the Lady Dawson! We shall miss your fine home and generous table."

"Back to Stratford, is it?"

Shakespeare paused his packing for a moment. "That is the question of the hour, Mrs. Dawson. What is a man of the theatre without a theatre? A horseman without a horse."

"What would you have me say to those who seek you?

Shakespeare shot her a look, wondering for a moment if she had heard anything. But that was unlikely. "If they are bearing a warrant, tell them I vanished into the night."

Mrs. Dawson thought that was quite amusing, and woke any of her tenants that might have been already asleep with her raucous laugh. "Oh, Mr. Shakespeare. Your wit is surely what I'll miss the most."

"You have been a fine audience. Mrs. Dawson. For those who do not appear to be seeking my arrest, you may tell them I have gone north."

"A man of mystery."

"Stratford is north, Mrs. Dawson."

"So Stratford it is then!"

"As are myriad other destinations, Mrs. Dawson. Suffice it to say north."

"So I shall Mr. Shakespeare. You have made me a conspirator."

An hour later, Mr. Shakespeare headed toward St. Paul's Cathedral, the center of London. If one wanted the news at midday, ambling up and down the center aisle you could hear it all. For excitement you could watch young men practice their archery shooting at birds unfortunate enough to have made their home in the interior. Yes, the many all too bright shafts of light that bled through the great stained glass windows were actually wounds from errant arrows.

At night, a different kind of commerce dominated. Thieves gathered to compare notes and select their next target, prostitutes found both customers and refuge, and various trades held office.

Trailed by a porter with his trunk, Shakespeare, approached a booth helmed by a dark man. Above the booth, barely visible, was a crude sign: Wagoners.

"Know of someone headed Stratford way, then?"

The dark man shook his head. "Not till light. Everyone knows that."

Shakespeare had fought enough for the day and let it pass. "How about charter?"

"You can always try the stables."

Even at this hour, a blacksmith brought showers of brilliant sparks as he pounded a new iron wheel rim into shape. London's paved streets near St. Paul's provided the transportation and commercial hub of the city, even at night. The stables were busy with horses arriving and leaving, being fed or organized into teams. Wagons clattered in all directions as businessmen and travelers struck bargains for goods and transportation.

As Shakespeare made his way toward the stables he suddenly saw a sight that seemed too magical to be true. Five fine green wagons, highlighted with lavish gold piping, some meant for freight, some for passengers, stood neatly in a line, ready for their horse teams to move into place. A sign painter was finishing his task on one of the wagons, working carefully by candlelight, as absorbed in his labors as if he were in some quiet studio instead in the middle of the road of a great metropolis.

Shakespeare drew close to examine the message.

'Pembroke's Men ~ Entertainments Direct from London'

Close by, in the shadows, a red-nosed man observed Shakespeare. "We have room for one more."

Shakespeare, startled, spun around, his hand on his dagger.

"Say you?"

Ben Bentley, the red-nosed promoter, laughed a little heh-heh-heh and held both his palms up, as if to say, 'No threat here.'

"Sorry to startle you, Will Shakespeare. I have seen you and I have seen your play."

Shakespeare shot back, "Which?"

Bentley was momentarily confused. "There is more than one? I thought you authored Henry of various parts."

Shakespeare didn't like being surprised in the dark, and the adrenaline was still coursing. "There is more. At least until we closed. Whose enterprise is this?"

Bentley closed his eyes in a slow blink, making a bow with his eyes, if not his body. "Mine. Ben Bentley's. In the service of his Lordship, Henry Herbert the Second, Earl of Pembroke, our esteemed patron."

"And you are headed?

"North. Ahead of the Death. Won't you join us? Burbage is already along."

This was surprising news. In the wake of the theatre closings, the established companies had broken up, and Shakespeare had assumed theatre, at least for the moment, was dead. But here was a company that had formed seemingly on the wing.

"Burbage? Really?"

"He will be here before dawn."

Shakespeare was momentarily perplexed. Without a company to write for, he would most likely not be writing dramas again. He had begun to flesh out his Stratford scenarios. Tending the land by day, children playing nearby as he enjoyed a smoke by the fire. Making adjustments to life with Anne, to the confinement of house, wife, field, and town.

"I have plans, actually."

Shakespeare's porter arrived, interrupting. "Here you are, sir." He indicated a coach not far away. There seemed to be a figure inside. "Headed north. Your baggage is on and belted."

Shakespeare thanked him and paid him off. He turned to Bentley. "When will you be returning to London?"

Bentley cocked his head as if the stars might provide the details of his plan. "End of summer. The Earl has promised us a new theatre on the south bank if we are allowed to reopen. For those that join us now, there will be shares."

Shakespeare heard that clearly. "Shares?"

Bentley confirmed. "Divided up."

"And where is your first town when you leave London?"

"Bedford."

Shakespeare hesitated, but he had so vividly envisioned the consequences of the closing of the theatre, of Marlowe's death, of the closing of everything that had thrilled him about London, that he was afraid. Afraid that in his desperate eagerness to not give up the glory of the theatre, that he would choose badly and without careful thought, join this pack of entertainers heading off on an unknowable, and dangerous, jaunt.

He was by nature a cautious man. He opened the door to his coach and dropped back into his seat. Shakespeare turned for a moment, saw Bentley watching him through the coach window, and turned away.

The teamster cried out, startling the horses as they momentarily slipped on the slick cobblestones, and then finding their footing, headed off into the night with the playwright aboard. From the confines of his coach, Shakespeare could see the occasional torch of tavern light pass by. But as poet and dramatist he could choose to see from whatever vantage point he fancied. And in this moment, he chose to hover above himself, standing on a high rooftop, stars above, London shimmering all around, and below, his own coach leading away with himself inside. Leaving not in triumph, but in the night, and possibly forever.

Thirteen — A Close Space

*B*ringing his consciousness back within himself, Shakespeare realized he wasn't alone in the coach. He turned and discreetly observed his seatmate, peering in the darkness, trying to see the face.

Eventually the flickers of light provided a patchwork of clues that could be pieced together. A female figure, all in black. A broad black hat, so broad that only one eye showed. And that eye was clearly evaluating him.

She spoke. "Actor."

She knew him, because the woman was Elinor. But Shakespeare didn't know her by this wardrobe nor by this voice. He was intrigued. "Yes?"

Elinor explained, pointed to herself and by way of identification, "Audience."

Shakespeare nodded. His eyes were adjusting to the darkness. "Aha."

Elinor explained further. "King Arthur."

"Oh, that one!" he chuckled. "By rights we should already have met, the audience was so sparse."

Elinor had good memories of the play. "I liked it. He, or rather, you, was quite amusing."

Shakespeare was pleased with her estimation. "I thought so as well. And now, apparently, there are two that share the opinion." He decided they had become intimate enough for him to disclose his name. It didn't seem particularly forward as she already knew it.

"Will."

"Elinor."

They jounced along in silence for a few moments. Elinor thought about explaining that she was also the doctor, the witness to Shakespeare and Marlowe at work. But then she decided against it. He seemed to have much on his mind, and she didn't want to make him think she had somehow tricked him when she was watching him at work.

Shakespeare then decided something that often happens when strangers cross paths on journeys with the likely expectation they will never see each other again. It seemed safe to use the coach as a confessional.

"I may have killed a man today."

That certainly broke the ice. Elinor, as doctor, had already heard a full spectrum of human surprises, and knew how to show none.

"May have?"

"I couldn't stay around to see the ultimate result."

Elinor couldn't help diagnosing. "What exactly did you do to him?"

If Shakespeare was surprised at the directness of her question, he didn't show it.

"I stuck him with my dagger."

"Where?"

For Shakespeare, the call to wordplay was even greater than that to swordplay might be for others. "In an eating-house."

Elinor shook her head.

Shakespeare demonstrated on himself, pointing somewhere close to his own appendix. "In the gut."

Elinor offered her diagnosis. "He might live. Might I ask what was the occasion?"

"He had murdered my friend. Christopher Marlowe."

Elinor was truly shocked. She had been quite charmed by Marlowe in the day she followed the two poets around. And she could immediately feel Shakespeare's great loss.

Shakespeare watched the flash of grief transform Elinor's face. "Now you look as though you have lost a friend."

Elinor explained as much as she felt necessary. "I admired his work. I am saddened for you and what you have lost."

"London will not be the same."

"May I ask where you are going?"

"You may. I think home to Stratford.

"Home."

She didn't ask it. Merely repeated.

But Shakespeare confirmed. "Indeed. And you? May I inquire as well?"

Elinor was not about to disclose that she was a doctor pursuing the tracks of the Black Death. "You may. I am traveling north on a personal matter.'

"Personal,' seems freighted with intrigue. Are you perhaps on a journey to murder someone yourself? Spring is an excellent season for revenge."

Elinor, knowing something of the poet's leaps, took him as being amusing, and laughed softly. "Not exactly."

Shakespeare was still enjoying his track. "I would have offered my dagger. It is fresh, tested and found not wanting."

"Many thanks."

"As a playsmith, I hold a license to ask."

"I doubt it, but I'll grant you one anyway."

Shakespeare mused over his choices. "Not murder, then. That leaves love. Assignation?"

"No."

Shakespeare was challenged. "Plots are running scarce. Collection of a debt, then?"

"Not."

"Aha. Power! You are on your way to overthrow an illegitimate royal of some sort."

"Hardly."

Shakespeare was stumped. "What then?"

Elinor was coyly beautiful. What could be better than to stump this lovely man?

"Secret."

Shakespeare feigned outrage. "I abhor secrets! Unless, of course, in a plot. Of my devising."

Elinor was pleased to have perplexed him. "So be it then."

Once again they rode along in silence, but everything had changed. They were becoming more than fellow travelers, but friends. Again. Just with a new identity for one of them.

Shakespeare's brow was furrowed as he puzzled over Elinor, and yet he was also enormously pleased at her very presence. And she, being a wise and serious person, was thinking deeply about what she wanted in life. She wanted her work to help solve the source of the plague. When her husband had died, when they were both so young, she had simply given up the notion that she might be ever be happy, or even married again. And yet, here she was, finding that the idea of happiness had stuck its foot in her door.

She looked over at Shakespeare. "Can I ask you another question?"

"I suspect these formalities will not last the night."

She wasn't clear what that meant.

"May I?"

"That was intended as an all-encompassing 'yes'."

"Let's not rush."

And then she looked surprised at herself. What in the world had she meant by that? Could she take the words back? She felt so foolish. "I mean we must keep our distances."

"Of course. Then 'yes' for this once."

"Good. With the theatres closed, might you be leaving London forever?"

"That is my thought. I must provide for my family and now I no longer see a way forward. So I may tend my flock, perhaps teach."

"That would be a loss."

"My writing was a means to an end. Actors need something to say. I gave it to them. Like shoes for feet."

"I thought it was more than that."

Was there a touch of bitterness here? "Perhaps. Sometimes shoes are more than shoes. Sometimes you can put on a pair and you feel that you might escape the pull of the earth."

Of course, knowing more about him than he knew she knew brought some urgency to her next question.

"And if you never wrote again? No one would see what you see."

Shakespeare let his own poet's sensibilities rise to the moment, and he allowed that spirit to play for a moment. "What I see is only what I see, and may be of no value."

She started to object, but he was only doing a little mental throat-clearing.

"I see dewdrops and planets. I see players, each in their own way, striving in their moment between first and last light. From mewling in their mother's milk to staggering off in old age, with mirth and mayhem along the way."

Shakespeare fell back in on himself. Returning to Stratford was a kind of little death, and he was saying goodbye to a part of life that had so enthralled him.

Elinor watched him, feeling his loss, her heart hurting.

Fourteen — The Turning Point

*T*he cow mooed softly. The gentle sound echoed around the inn's courtyard, announcing that breakfast was on offer for guests of the Turning Point. Townspeople came by to offer breads and meats. The innkeeper's daughter brought draughts of morning beer. The sun was beginning to burn through a cold morning fog.

Elinor sat on a bench, sipping tea and reading a thick text. Shakespeare studied her, circled to see another view. She was aware of him without seeming to have looked up.

"Are you imagining me as a specimen, Mr. Shakespeare?"

He came closer, and, graceful as a cat, seated himself opposite her. "I am indeed. You are a model of a sort."

"Oh?"

"I am contemplating whether you might preferably create the form for a great hero in a tragedy or else a comedy. Your wit would suffice either way."

She closed her book and smiled, amused. "I would prefer comedy, having had enough of the other." And then she wondered if he was really still in playwright mode. "I thought you were abandoning the quill."

"I am. Or am about to. The habit dies hard."

Elinor thought she had a helpful notion. "You could write for a small circle of friends. They would be delighted, I am sure."

"So I could! How gratifying." The thought depressed him. "How modest in every way."

He stared at her as if he might discern the answer he sought in her beauty. He knew the answer was there, but felt he might be afraid to acknowledge it.

He finally explained. "I confess. I am torn."

Elinor was a profoundly rational person. If there was a problem, she would find a methodology for solving it. And then accept whatever solution resulted. "How will you know?"

Shakespeare frowned. "I could wait for a sign…"

Magically, a rooster answered his request with a timely dawn salute. This only emboldened him.

"…in the call of a cock." He put his hands out to her. "I could seek the help of others…" and then he pulled his open palms back, bringing them together in the gesture of prayer. "Or look for an answer from a deity." His hand went from prayer to shielding his eyes from the brilliance of the Lord. But then he peeked at her to see how he was doing.

Elinor laughed. What could be more delightful than being entertained by this man?

Encouraged, he let his improvisation take a dark turn, conjuring up a storm with a sweep of his cloak. "Or, I could wait for Fate — a sudden squall, an accident: a limb falls across the road, blocking my path toward one of two destinies."

Elinor saw an opening for logic. "Where would you prefer that Fate caused that limb to fall?"

Shakespeare did not need to ponder it. "The road to Stratford, in truth."

"There you have it."

And so he did.

And yet did not. She had just pointed him the way he wanted to go, but "There is more to it than that."

"There always is. If we consider everything, we would venture nothing. The question is, what ought one to consider if every possibility cannot be pleased."

"And you have an answer to that thicket?"

"Only for myself and the choices I needed to make. I would not presume to alter another's course."

Shakespeare couldn't resist the dramatic. He brought himself to his knee in front of her, pleaded perhaps too dramatically, "Alter mine."

"The heart has its own wisdom."

That seemed to help. He didn't say what he had decided, but he seemed ready to do something, and began to stride away. And then he paused, having forgotten something.

"Thanks, then, dear lady."

She nodded in response. "To your path, whatever it may be."

"And yours, " he rejoined. "May they cross."

Fifteen — On the Road to Bedford

*T*he glorious caravan was in the London darkness no more. Five splendid bright green wagons, each drawn by a pair of fine fast horses wearing fabulous red feather bridle plumes, roared through the countryside packed with actors, costumes, props, and draperies. The dramatic parade was calculated to stir the blood of any town it might storm into.

Standing at the front of the lead coach, each hanging on to an outside grip, Shakespeare and Burbage ignored whatever danger there might be, so absorbed were they in their conversation. The driver was seated between them, and they yelled over his head.

"We're going to have a different audience, Richard. Our London people were seeing two or three plays a week. They're sharp."

Burbage was thinking about that, too. "Yes, we knew what else they were seeing and talking about, no question. They were feeding on us and us on them"

"Competition was good for us. Johnson wrote a clever play, and we only had weeks to top it."

"It worried me sometimes. That the grounders were getting too damn smart for us. They walked in ready to be bored."

"Bored and dangerous, with food in hand."

Burbage nodded. "I'm thinking of Peele's 'Device of the Pageant'"

Shakespeare spit for luck. "Wretched piece."

Burbage spat for luck, too. "Wretched indeed. They were selling those damned new candied apples. Brained one of our best youngsters."

"Terrible business. No question."

Burbage was wondering where Shakespeare was going with this. "And now we're bringing London theatre to the great backwaters of England. Throw out our old plays?"

Shakespeare wasn't sure. "I'm thinking we need to know for whom we're playing, and maybe tone down the long speeches."

Burbage agreed. "Perforce."

Shakespeare was thinking about the people he grew up with in Stratford, when theatre companies would come through. "Less ribaldry. They are more likely to be decent folk."

Burbage added that to his mental checklist. "Less ribaldry."

Shakespeare was remembering. "And more swordplay. Even if they couldn't understand the story they loved the flash of great steel and mighty tintinnerations."

Burbage agreed and added, "And a little blood goes a long away."

"And a lot goes even further."

The driver who seemed to be asleep during most of this suddenly started. He'd seen the first signs of town. "Get out the drums!"

The call was carried and repeated from coach to coach.

Shakespeare and Burbage peered ahead, trying to see what the driver had seen.

The driver called out. "Bedford Town, round the bend."

As the caravan rolled into Bedford, it became readily apparent that an attraction of considerable importance had preceded the players. Townspeople and visitors, distinguished by their broad hats and carrying enough food for a couple of days, were drawn toward the town's commons. When the green wagons came to a stop in the Bedford Inn courtyard, they were barely able to capture enough room so that they would be able to unhitch the horses.

The innkeeper kept busy dashing here and there, yelling orders to his various harried charges, simultaneously greeting customers, and leading a pair of horses to his stables.

Ben Bentley leapt from the second coach and looked around for someone in charge. The innkeeper recognized the look and approached Bentley, still guiding the two horses.

"Looking for me?"

Bentley sized him up. "If you are the proprietor."

The innkeeper told Bentley there were no rooms left. Not here and not anywhere else for miles around.

"What is the grand event?"

"We've a hanging tomorrow, a notorious murderer, and the crowds have come from far and wide. I may be able to find some canvas, arrange some kind of tents for tonight. Hopefully it won't rain."

"And the horses?"

"We can take care of them."

"And will it be possible to set up our theatre in the courtyard? Will bring you a great many customers."

"Aye. After the man is hung, your show can follow. But you'll be needing to see the mayor for your warrant to perform."

Bentley and Shakespeare went off in search of the mayor, and soon found him at Moot Hall, a two-story timbered brick building that offered a good view of the gathering crowd across the dusty town square.

A long line of merchants waited as the mayor signed permits and accepted fees, which went directly into the purse that hung at his waist.

With theatrical self-importance Bentley swept past the line and addressed the mayor directly.

"Is this the office where a theatre company can procure a performance warrant?"

Without looking up, the mayor ordered Bentley into the line. "Take your place, man!"

"But we have much to do! Stages to build, announcements to be made…"

"Back of the line! If you will!"

Bentley turned red and blustered about, while Shakespeare observed, bemused. When their turn finally came, the mayor looked at Bentley for the first time, and took in Shakespeare as well.

"Theatre people, eh? And who said we allow godless distractions in this village?"

"We were told that the people of Bedford value culture. We are London's finest, sponsored by His Eminence, The Right Earl of Pembroke."

"Never heard of 'im. Nevertheless, even high culture has its price. A crown for each performance day."

Bentley counted out his coins. "We will be playing for four days. I'll come back if our engagement is extended."

The mayor took a warrant from under his desk pad. "This is your warrant for four days. No animal baiting, no wagering, no prostitution of any sort, no libel, no appealing to the lowest forms of human depravity."

Shakespeare was eager to hear more about the latter prohibition. "Can you enumerate those for us?"

But Bentley interrupted. "That won't be necessary! Thank you, m'lord."

Bentley turned to leave, but Shakespeare had something more on his mind.

"Lord Mayor?"

"Mister…"

"Shakespeare. I have a request.

The mayor's hand automatically sprung to open the maw of his purse.

"We are receptive to requests."

"You have the condemned man here in Bedford?"

"We do. John Parker."

"Would you mind if I interviewed him?"

There was the clear sound of a coin clinking into the mayor's purse. But the mayor seemed not to notice.

Shakespeare continued. "I would like to understand his cast of mind."

Another clink, but the mayor was yet unresponsive.

"As a theatre person."

Another clink. That one seemed to do the trick. The mayor seemed satisfied. "I can't see the harm."

"Please advise the jailer."

Shakespeare swept a low bow and backed out of the room.

Sixteen — The First Stage

The two green wagons that carried the stage and draperies stood horseless as the men, including every actor, unloaded massive trestles and boards.

Because the company was new, the boards were fresh. The clever design was intended to make it possible to assemble and disassemble the stage within a few hours, all with the use of pegs to hold everything together. Being new, the pegs were still green, and a bit oversized. Without prodigious amounts of swearing, very little would have been accomplished.

The drapers carefully unfolded their fabulous new drapes and hung them on the frames they had already assembled. The gold and red drapes behind the stage served two purposes — to be a backdrop for the stage itself and secondly to provide an enclosed backstage for costume changes. This enclosed space, the tiring house, was where anyone not on stage during a performance could retreat.

A good-sized crowd had gathered to enjoy the spectacle, and to offer helpful advice when the workers puzzled over a piece of their new equipment.

"Why don't you get a bigger mallet?"

"If I do, I'll be putting these pegs somewhere else. And you won't like it."

Kemp, the company's versatile comic lead, intuited that it might be a better idea to entertain the crowd than to antagonize them. He flipped head over heels to where the front of the stage was taking shape, produced some large lawn bowling pins, and began to juggle as he danced a fancy jig, all the while making patter about the upcoming shows.

As Shakespeare worked alongside the stagehands, he surveyed the setting in the inn courtyard. His gaze went from Kemp's shenanigans to the delighted crowd that gathered around him. And then, suddenly, he saw her in the crowd with her eyes upon him. He was startled at the sudden grip in his chest, and turned away from her to gather himself. He raised a mallet and pounded on a peg. And then he looked up at where she had been, expecting her image to have been a mirage. But it wasn't. And she was still staring.

He leapt off the stage and walked up to her. He was sweaty and dusty. She was as fresh as a mowed lawn.

Elinor spoke first. "Not Stratford, then."

Shakespeare shook his head. "No. You turned my head. And you? Your secrets are here in Bedford?"

"Partly."

Shakespeare gazed at her, but no more answers were going to be forthcoming. "You are staying here?"

"I am."

"May I ask you to join the company at our table? I must warn you, before you accept, a theatre company can tend toward mayhem without provocation."

"I accept. I am honored."

"We have a rehearsal coming up for a play we're working on. Care to observe?"

Seventeen — A Rough Draft

*B*y nightfall the tap room would be the center of public activity at the Bedford Inn, where fresh barrels of brew would be rolled in, hoisted to their racks and tapped with maple mallets.

For the benefit of the Pembroke's Company, a fresh cask had been brought over, and the men had gathered to catch the first pint, not knowing the beer had just rolled and bounced across a hot and rocky path.

The publican, wearing a neck-to-foot canvas smock, let the men draw near with excitement as he drew his mallet back. Thirst was in air the, and thirst he would slake.

Bang! The mallet struck the bung, driving it into the keg, followed by a shower of warm, smelly beer, soaking the actors.

Shakespeare sheltered a sheaf of freshly copied parts as the men wiped themselves off with whatever they could find. One of the boys brought a tankard over to him. "Late breakfast, M'lord?"

Shakespeare handed out the sheets to those who could read. "These characters are not your kings and queens and lords and so on. These are everyday folk trying to not simply entertain their betters, but to delight them by putting on a play. But they are working way above their station, and can only guess what might delight."

Kemp piped up. "Sounds like us."

Shakespeare didn't disagree. "Maybe it is. And if so, even a little, then we should play it well. Can we start with Peter Quince, who is a carpenter in actual fact, as he assigns a part in the play to Flute, who I have made a bellows-mender."

Richard Burbage took every opportunity to gently tease the young playwright, as if he were a genius of some kind. "Flute? Blow? Bellows? By Heaven, you've outdone yourself, young Will."

"I believe it will play in Bedford. Depending on the players. Shall we give it a run?"

As he began to explain what he was looking for, Elinor came into the room and settled herself in a corner. Highly aware of her presence, Shakespeare occasionally glanced in her direction to see if he could read her thoughts.

Burbage took up his character of Peter Quince and began to read. "Flute, you must take Thisbe on you."

John Wickham, young, reed-thin and a naturally high voice that time would never lower, became the character Flute. "What is Thisbe? A wandering knight?"

Burbage, as Peter Quince, explained how it was going to be. "It is the lady that Pyramus must love."

Flute was alarmed. "Nay, faith, let me not play a woman; I have a beard coming."

Burbage dropped out of character for laughs. "You're going to be Thisbe, you wee shit, or I'll have your nethers!"

The company thought that was hilarious. Shakespeare winced. "Not exactly what is on the page."

Burbage returned to character. "You shall play it in a mask, and you may speak as small as you will."

Wickham looked at Shakespeare. "What kind of a small voice did you have in mind?"

Shakespeare screwed up his face and pressed his lips together so even when he tried to speak the opening was tiny, as if being asked to kiss a skunk. "Like this…"

Wickham gave it a go. "Asleep my love? What. Dead, my dove? Dead, dead? A tomb must cover thy sweet eyes."

Shakespeare stepped in. "You need bigger gestures. As your voice is small, your motion must be large." He gave an example, swooning over the dead Thisbe and throwing himself about the imaginary stage.

Wickham asked, "And then I stab myself?"

Shakespeare assented. "Yes, after you finish the rest of the speech, if it so please you."

Wickham continued to Thisbe's end. "And farewell, friends; Thus Thisbe ends: Adieu, adieu, adieu."

Shakespeare applauded lightly, frustrated. "And that's about it. We can make it broader, some falling down. Maybe a costume should rip."

Burbage tried to be helpful. He opened his shirt and appeared to lose control of his imaginary huge breasts. "Melons fall out? Always good for something."

Shakespeare frowned. "I am not persuaded."

Kemp jumped in. "Maybe it's us. Maybe it's the way we're playing it."

Shakespeare wasn't sure, since he was looking for something that until now had never existed. "Not at all, Kemp. You are flesh and blood, but when you utter my lines, what I have written drains the life out of you."

Shakespeare turned to Elinor. "Your thoughts?"

Elinor wanted to be supportive. "I thought it was very sad."

Shakespeare winced. "Lovely. I thought I had scripted comedy."

At that moment two porters arrived with massive trays of food.

Shakespeare turned to his group. "Carry on without me, or give it up for a while. I've got an errand."

He bid farewell for the moment to Elinor, as well. "Until dinner, then?"

And he led the two porters away from the inn.

Eighteen — The Gates of Hell

The Bedford jail provided one of two centers of focus for the throngs that had been drawn to Bedford for the hanging, the other being the construction of the gallows not far away.

Shakespeare, his porters, and their food worked their way amongst the spectators, vendors, merrymakers, and children, all hoping to get a glimpse of the condemned.

A low wall surrounding the jail enclosed a patch of dirt, and a miserable woman sat there, chained and guarded. Shakespeare and entourage arrived at the jail itself, where the keeper was expecting them.

The keeper indicated the woman and explained. "That's the wife of the victim, and the instigator of it all, if you're interested."

Shakespeare was, and marched his team towards her. "And you are?"

She was unable to speak. A guard nearest to her spoke for her. "She is Mrs. Brewer."

Shakespeare raised his voice, as if, in grief, she might have become hard of hearing. "Mrs. Brewer, I am bringing a meal for John Parker. Would you like some food?"

She looked up, her once blue but now gray eyes looking in the general direction of Shakespeare, and took a single fig from the proffered tray.

Inside the jail, a table was brought in and set with a grand feast, considering the circumstances. The condemned, John Parker, overcame his disbelief and began to eat, tearing into a roasted fowl. Shakespeare waited and watched, giving the gift of the appearance of infinite time to one who had very little remaining.

Eventually, Parker was feeling adequately stuffed and was ready to talk with his benefactor. Outside, Jane, his beloved, could be heard sobbing from time to time, through the barred window.

Parker began, "Thank you for this fine spread."

"You are indeed welcome, Mr. Parker. I would prefer we'd have met under different stars, but we did not."

"Different stars. Would they were."

Shakespeare gestured with the decanter. "More wine?"

Parker took some and sipped.

"So was it stars? Was it Fate that you and the goldsmith's wife became lovers?"

Parker had never been asked to think before. He was silent as he tried his choices. Then, "How can I say what it was?" Then he thought some more. "There was something from the first time I looked up and there she was. I couldn't even look away." Parker concentrated, rethinking the moment. "But she was married…"

Shakespeare sought refinement. "Did you know that then?"

"No. She explained over time. She was young. He was old and cared little for her. We noticed each other when I brought my produce in from the farm, and we talked about radishes and carrots and such. It was her voice. I was lost to her."

"Vegetables."

"We were strongly attracted. Before long she asked me to bring the wagon to the back of their place, and bring whatever I had to the scullery."

"Did you kiss her then?"

"And had her, too."

Again, Shakespeare sought clarification. There would be no opportunity for a return visit. "The first time you came to the back?"

"There didn't seem to be a reason to wait. We could tell where things were headed."

"Did you think what might happen if her husband found out?"

"She said not to worry, he wouldn't care. Then one day, when I asked her to leave him and come be on my farm, she said he would never let her. She said her dowry had paid for the gold he used in his trade, and she would lose it all if she left."

Shakespeare observed, with as much neutrality as he could muster, "So you killed him?"

Parker was offended. "Not! That's not how it happened. I gave up on the idea of her ever coming with me."

"So how did you come to murder him?"

"It was an accident, as I swore with my oath."

Shakespeare was thinking about his own recent experience when he had a dagger in his hand. "Accidents do indeed happen. How did yours come about?"

Parker put himself back in witness mode. Maybe this man could somehow, magically, save him if he simply told it the right way this time. "We were in bed, as we often were. Such delights."

Distracted by Jane's sobbing outside, he cried to her, "I love you Darling. We'll be together forever, soon enough."

Then, back to his inquisitor. "Mr. Brown walks in, and he's already carrying a dagger, and he goes for me. I have my wits about me and clobber him with the lamp nearby, and now he's on the floor, head bleeding, not moving too much. So I ran him through."

This was the moment Shakespeare had been seeking, the one he sensed would be there, and where he could make his discovery. How to slow everything down and make some space?

"How were you standing?"

Parker was still visualizing the scene he had been describing. He looked around and saw exactly where Brown had been. Parker himself was a big man and powerful.

"I knew there was a knife not far away."

Shakespeare noticed a large carving knife that had come with the food. He casually offered it to the murderer.

"Something like this one?"

Parker took it and tested its balance. "Pretty close. So there I was, and there he was."

"What were you thinking?"

Parker looked at him as if Shakespeare might be mad. "Thinking!?"

Shakespeare just stared back.

"I was thinking to kill 'im."

Not what Shakespeare was looking for. "Did you see yourself?"

Parker was momentarily mystified by the question. He dropped his posture of murder and suddenly recalled something — something so real and clear, it flooded back to him.

"I saw the gates of Hell open for me."

"You did?"

"I did. I said, 'John Parker, the man is down, he ain't going to kill you at the moment, and you can leave him here.'"

"You said that?"

Parker explained, "To myself. You couldn't a heard it even if you was standing right by me."

"And did you say anything else to yourself?"

"In fact, I did. I said, 'But you love her, and he'll not let you have her.' And so I run him straight through."

"And how long did all this take? From seeing the gates of Hell to deciding to run him through?"

Parker went back into his original position, knife high above his head, ready to plunge. "From here…"

He hesitated for a split second. And then killed Brown once more. "To here."

Shakespeare got it. He had helped Parker to escape, not the gallows, but being a victim of fate.

Slowing it down, he had seen everything. "The whole world in the blink of an eye."

Parker wiped the imaginary blood off the real knife and carefully placed it back on the table.

He concurred. "That is the truth."

Nineteen — The Company at Repast

At the Bedford Inn, anticipation of a hanging had put the large crowd in a raucous mood. At the grand center table the Pembroke's Men were in a world of their own. Burbage was the big man, hosting at one end of the grand board. At the other was comic Kemp, always good for a witty imitation, a funny face or a loud punchline. Midway were Shakespeare and Elinor, and across from them Bentley the impresario, looking worried as always. Several teenage boys who played the female and children's roles were carefully silent at the table, not wanting to call attention to themselves as they sipped their beers and slipped into a tipsy haze.

Although there were other women in the inn, at the Pembroke table Elinor was the only female. Although she wasn't yet aware of it, most of the actors were performing for her benefit, and to 'support' Will.

Waiters arrived with mighty platters of food, and everyone helped themselves with whatever tools were available, mostly hands and knives. Shakespeare, ever the gentleman, grabbed a leg of something as it went by, inspected it carefully for unwelcome hangers-on, and placed it on Elinor's plate.

Burbage clanged on his vessel and stood to make a toast. "To Will Shakespeare, for his great courage in joining this merry band…"

He was interrupted by many "Hear, hears" from the company.

He continued, "May we benefit from his wit and wisdom with at least one new play before our journey is done."

There were more assents in the form of grunts and grumblings.

Burbage had more. "And more importantly, to this lady who has shown up here we know not how…"

Kemp sang out from the other end of the table, "An act of God, no doubt."

"May the beautiful Dark Lady…" Burbage went on, but Shakespeare interjected, "Elinor. Of London."

"May the beautiful Elinor, then, bring us great luck." And then, seeking a rhyme to close a couplet, "and to Shakespeare, hereby, a great…"

Kemp saved the day, jumping in with, "Good fortune!"

Laughter followed all around. Burbage aimed his superb voice all the way to Elinor with theatrical intimacy, as if only the two of them were present. "Did you know he was a playwright?"

"I have seen some. Henry the Fourth."

Burbage was now on solid ground and could build his edifice for young Will. "Marvelous history. Marvelous." A pause to ready his chest of pearls. "Did you know he was a tragedian as well?"

Elinor hesitated. "No, I …"

Burbage opened his arms to pave the way for the treasure to come. "One of the greatest of our season."

Ben Bentley was mystified. He thought he knew what Shakespeare had already presented on the London stage. "And among these plays are?"

Burbage looked shocked that Bentley could be so ignorant. "Right up there with Dr. Faustus." Somehow Kemp was in on it, and announced with Burbage, like two trumpets heralding from opposite ends of the table, "Titus Andronicus."

Shakespeare was puzzled as to whether they were having him on or not. He smelled a rat. He quietly explained to Elinor, "Something I was working on last year. Nothing to mention."

But Elinor was both curious and polite. And so it came to be that she uttered the Question That Should Not Be Asked. "Really? What's it about?"

Burbage stepped into the breech. "Where to begin? Titus is about to become Roman emperor, as thanks for his war against the Goths. Titus doesn't feel worthy of accepting the role. But when he does return to Rome, he brings with him Tamora, the captured queen."

Kemp jumped in. "With her three sons."

Another voice at the table added, "And don't forget Elon, the Moorish one…"

Shakespeare was going to sit back and let this blow over, but was drawn out by the error. "Sorry, that's Aaron."

Kemp managed to speak even though he had just taken a huge bite of roast, "And Aaron would turn out to be the secret lover of Tamora."

Burbage took over the narrative, all still directed at entertaining Elinor. "Will's tale becomes complex when Titus decides it would be a capital idea to kill one of Tamora's children…"

Kemp filled in, "Alarbus — we don't see a lot of him…"

Shakespeare decided to try and cut it off. "Thank you so much, gentlemen." And to Elinor, "And that's about it. Pass the wine, please."

But Burbage plowed on, ever more vivid, knowing the gore to come. "Naturally enough, the remaining sons, Demetrius and Chiron want revenge." Burbage took a moment to think about Shakespeare's playcrafting. "Young Will puts a fair amount of reliance on revenge, come to think of it. If I were you," he said for Elinor's edification, "I would take great care before crossing him. Unless it were ab-so-lute-ly necessary."

Elinor took in the advice in great earnestness. "Do not provide Mr. Shakespeare cause for revenge. Noted."

This brought amusement from the company. Another actor, a swarthy sort, continued the narrative. "In the meanwhile the wretch who does become king, Saturninus, wants to marry Lavinia, who is daughter of Titus. Titus says fine, but Lavinia is already spoken for by Saturninus's brother, Bassianus."

The actor interrupted himself to ask as an aside to Will, "Where do you get these names? What kind of anus is Bassi-anus?"

Shakespeare shrugged. He took a quick glance to see how Elinor was enjoying being the audience for this.

The swarthy one, rolled on, "But Bassianus refuses to give Lavinia up."

Kemp took up the thread. "Then it begins to get a little hot-blooded. Titus gets in a fight with one of his offspring and kills him, and the king gets his hackles up with Titus. And then things settle down."

Elinor takes a sip of wine. "Thank goodness."

Burbage extended his index finger in the classic "wait" gesture. "Until the next day. Aaron gets Demetrius and Chiron to kill Bassianus, so they can rape Lavinia. To keep her quiet…" he grimaced for effect… "they cut out her tongue."

Elinor appeared to be having some difficulty in enjoying the story. "What!?"

Robbie jumped in to explain the obvious. "So she won't tell who did it."

To Kemp it seemed logical, too. "Naturally."

Elinor took a long fresh look at Will. Re-evaluating. "You? Wrote? This?"

Given the time and place, Shakespeare could have explained how the play might work in the theatre. He could have explained that the audiences that season were hungry for gore, primed by the bear-baiting events down the street that the theatres were forced to compete with. He could have explained that when it's a play up on the stage people don't think it's as real as it seemed to be as told here by his intoxicated players.

But this wasn't the time or place to explain. All he could manage was, "Well, there's more…"

And Burbage figured it couldn't hurt to add a fillip of what he considered flattery. "Not only did he write it, but he played Chiron so well that the audience was screaming for his arrest after he cut out Lavinia's tongue."

Elinor suddenly stood. "I'm so sorry, but I have lost my appetite."

And with that she removed herself from the table, found a way out, and disappeared into the night.

The swarthy one was somewhat frustrated. "We didn't even get to the part about chopping off her hands."

Shakespeare nodded in sardonic agreement. "Not everyone is a connoisseur of the theatre."

And with that, he rushed out to find her, and make amends.

Twenty — The Stars, the Stables, a Horse

William searched the courtyard, then walked the perimeter of the building. When he returned by way of the stables, there Elinor was, communing with a horse who also seemed to appreciate the visit.

"Elinor, I must apologize."

She did not turn around to face him. "For what?"

"For the men, the Company, the lack of tenderness."

She turned toward him with a slight smile. "I can take it."

"You can?"

"Indeed. I saw the play."

Shakespeare was amazed. His poetic gifts abandoned him. "You did?"

Elinor nodded. "Twice."

And Shakespeare was twice stunned. "No."

His mind raced back through dinner, reassessing her seeming outrage.

"Then why did you…"

"Because I wanted you here."

The poet still lacked for words. "Oh."

Because there really was no more need for words, they were about to kiss. But the horse got to her first.

Shakespeare offered an alternative. "I was able to get a room."

"Me too."

"I must caution that I share my room with at least four others."

"Let's visit mine."

Twenty-One — A Midsummer's Night

The moonlight found the lovers catching their breath. The sound of the night was as richly textured as the blackness itself: in the quiet of their room they could hear laughter and voices coming up from the dining room below. Somewhere in the night a madrigal was being sung. The horses whinnied in the stables.

Elinor perched herself on top of Shakespeare so she could stare at him by moonlight. Her neck was bare, and from time to time she kissed him because it was pleasant to do so.

Shakespeare stared at her, too. "I see beauty beyond comprehension,"

"I see an extraordinary man."

"I want to be here, just like this, until time comes to a standstill."

Elinor considered this. "We would starve."

"I don't mind."

"Neither do I."

Shakespeare thought about how it might be. "They would find us here, just like this."

"I don't care."

"The inn will fade from all memory. A seed from the chestnut outside this window will find a moist spot in the earth. The sun will warm it, and the tree will entwine itself around our memory, creating a bower where our bed now lies. And when two lovers climb our tree and find our bower, they will fall in love forever…"

"Is that what this is?"

"As I was saying: In love forever, just as we are."

She smiled and kissed him yet again. "Apologies for the interruption."

"And so, in the world, there will always be lovers almost as fine as this."

"But not quite as…"

"No. Not quite as, because they will say we were the greatest love the world had ever known."

Elinor wondered what it might take to make that come true. "Only if you write it. There is no one else who can."

"Hmm. But then we couldn't stay here forever."

"I could bring your quill to bed."

There was no pun he could ignore. "I did."

Elinor smiled softly. "Indeed. And therefore, you should write again."

"And he did."

And they began to make love all over again.

Twenty-Two — A Midsummer Night's Morning

*I*n the dim light of dawn, Shakespeare slowly came to consciousness, remembered where he was and with whom, turned to gaze upon her and instead discovered he was eye-to-eye with the Doctor's plague mask.

"Zounds!"

Elinor was dressing. "I meant to tell you."

Shakespeare was still recovering from the shock. He was not awake enough to be sure whether she was real or a metaphor of some kind. "Are you Death?"

"I hope not. I am a doctor. I follow the Black Death."

"You are a doctor?" He begin to sort back through his final days in London. Click, click, click. Click. "Are you also my friend, the doctor?"

"You and Marlowe?"

"Yes. That one! Please don the mask!"

Elinor did so and waggled her head for his benefit.

"I see! How stupid of me!"

He pulled her into bed, kissed as much of her as he could get to, and tried to kiss her on the mouth.

But the mask's long nose gave whoever might want it considerable leverage over the movement of the wearer's head. Being kissed with the mask made Elinor feel as if she had lost control. Because she loved him it was funny, not frightening. But it quickly became overwhelming. "Stop! Stop!"

He gave her a moment to catch her breath. She finally did and contemplated him through the beady eyes of the mask.

Shakespeare began to re-engage his poet brain. "Love is…"

Elinor had no problem finishing his thought. "Myopic. That's the word. Love is myopic."

He contemplated his beloved in her frightening mask. "And sometimes better for it."

Twenty-Three — Setting the Stage

O n market days, the Bedford market was a gathering place for farmers and craftspeople from the surrounding area to set up their stands. It was a place to share news, and watch the children make new friends.

But today was different. At the center of the square, a group of rowdy craftsmen was busy building a stage of some kind, and a crowd watched, commented on their progress, and picnicked as they held their spaces for the great event. Kemp wore a sandwich board for 'Pembroke's Men" and juggled for the crowd's delight.

As Shakespeare surveyed the scene, he noticed Elinor in her mask and black robe as she moved quietly among the crowd. She was also observing, but looking for signs of something extremely specific.

Rats scampered among the crowd, fighting for scraps. When someone noticed one, it would be shooed away, as one might a stray cat. For a time Elinor carefully observed a baby in its basket on the ground. When the mother raised the baby's blanket to check on her, Elinor could see telltale tiny red dots of flea bites on the child's arm.

Shakespeare found a spot of shade and watched the stage intently. Niles the *Bestboy* 'supervised the activity on the gallows, where several men fussed with the trapdoor. "More grease on the budgie! We don't want any hiccups, now do we?"

Niles surveyed the crowd, impressed by the size of it. He turned to his men, but spoke loudly enough that the masses could hear him.

"This!"

Like a stage manager, Niles was testing both the instrument, in this instance his own voice, and the acoustics of the performance space. He paused and surveyed the audience, judged that he was being heard.

Satisfied, he continued. "This! This is a serious business."

Some of the crew nodded, hesitated, pondered, and then continued with whatever work they were doing before.

But Niles wasn't finished. "A man is to have his life ended here today, on this stage."

Again, the men had an ear cocked toward him, but continued in their labors.

"A man. A man like any of us."

For one of the carpenters, Sawyer, that was too much. "Maybe like you. But not like me."

And another carpenter agreed. "He's right there, Niles. The man's a murderer and deserves to die."

Niles was searching to put his finger on the meaning of it all. He was full of portent, but had not yet found the words he wanted. "Yes but and yes but. The man is a man, and we are men. And that makes him like any other. To some extent. And here…"

He gestured to the scaffold, rising high against the sky. "And here his neck will be tested and found wanting."

Niles gave his impression of what was about to happen, with a snap of his neck and a terrible grimace. A collective breath was drawn in, and Niles was secretly pleased with his efforts.

Niles turned to his crew working on the trapdoor. "Are we ready to test our craft?"

The men generally said 'yes' and backed away from their handiwork.

Niles addressed a small young man who nervously shifted his weight from foot to foot. "Billy. Are you ready?"

Billy nodded, ambled over to the rope, and placed it around his neck. The crowd grew anxious, fearing what might happen next.

Niles was smiling in a comforting, encouraging way. "All set?"

Billy had his hands up around the rope and nodded wanly.

Niles shifted into high drama mode. "And now, in the name of the Queen, I condemn thee to meet thy Maker, whoever that might be…"

And with that Niles gave the signal, and one of the workers swung a mighty mallet at the 'budgie.' The trapdoor dropped away and Billy dropped through. Then the rope pulled taut, Billy's body jerked, and he began to swing back and forth.

The crowd gasped. Shakespeare watched its reaction with particular attention to Elinor's masked body language.

The workmen rushed over to the trap door and peered down at Billy. For a moment, then two, then three, he didn't move. A single scream was heard from the crowd.

There was a flurry of workmen around Billy, where he hung, without motion.

Unfortunately, the workers had neglected to have a bench at the ready nearby so they could easily get to Billy and free him. He dangled there for too long.

"He's dead! For God's sake, cut him down!"

"Where's the damn knife?"

Finally, a worker dragged a stool over and sawed away at the rope, while another tried to raise Billy and take pressure off his neck.

Elinor came forward, trying to get close enough to help.

The rope was cut through, and Billy dropped to the ground at Elinor's feet. She rolled back one of his eyelids, and saw some motion.

"He's alive!"

Then Billy wriggled, bringing cheers.

Niles brought his men together to the stage and led them in a bow. Or tried to. Not all of them knew what a bow was, so some joined in and some didn't understand they had been part of a theatrical performance.

Niles announced to the crowd, "Our labors here are justly concluded."

Elinor put her ear to Billy's chest and listened carefully for a moment. "Now listen, young man. You've had a close call. I'm a doctor, so if you start fainting or can't catch your breath, you come find me at the inn. Promise?"

Billy nodded that he understood, and Elinor turned away to find Will standing nearby, taking it all in.

Twenty-Four — A Comedy of Errors

*T*he hanging had gone well for all, even, considering the circumstances, for poor John Parker who at least had been dispatched at the first try and with little of the bouncing and jouncing that can be so disturbing if you are witnessing your first. Many had stayed around to watch Parker be cut down and then had come over to the inn, seeking refreshment.

The crowd at the Inn was still exchanging minute observations about the hanging. Some were pleased that he had died quickly. Others expressed their disappointment that he hadn't jumped around more before becoming still. After all, they had come so far.

Many of the children were still wide-eyed. Though none were naïve regarding death, the shock of seeing a healthy man suddenly go still was profound. Others were still screaming, and, truth be told, some of the parents found their terror worthy of mirth.

And more mirth was in the air. What better to soothe these raw emotions but with a comedy?

"Why, how now, Dromio! Where runn'st thou so fast?"

Shakespeare was onstage, wearing make-up, warm in the late afternoon sun that heated the inn's courtyard.

The play was the very first performance by Pembroke's Men, and a feeling of newness pervaded. The costumes were beautiful and fresh; the draperies behind the stage were brilliant and without wear. The actors were bright and eager, delighted to be performing again, enjoying enormously the novelty of being on their fresh boards en plein air.

The setting was truly theatre in the round, for the audience had gathered not just in every available space within the courtyard and three of the stage's four sides. But even behind the stage lucky guests crowded into the courtyard's upper windows to enjoy an apparently free entertainment dropped under their lucky noses.

Elinor was in middle of the audience, and Shakespeare, playing Antipholus, couldn't help but lock eyes with her from time to time. Kemp was playing Dromio, Antipholus's servant, trying to understand why he has been mistaken for someone else. "Do you know me, sir? Am I Dromio? Am I your man? Am I myself?"

"Thou art Dromio, thou art my man, thou art thyself."

Dromio tries to explain that something has gone wrong in his universe. "Marry, sir, besides myself, I am due to a woman; one that claims me, one that haunts me, one that will have me."

There was some commotion offstage that led to a pause in the action on it. Members of the audience had their attention directed to an unscripted scene taking place in one of the courtyard windows. As a couple watched the play from the comfort of their room, Ben Bentley barged in and demanded money from them. More of the audience watched the excellent pantomime revealing that the couple thought they were in their rights to watch the play for free. But Bentley expressed his disagreement by reaching out and slamming the heavy shutters closed.

Shakespeare frowned before resuming the play, improvising to pick up the thread.

"The woman you are due to. Then she bears some breadth?

Kemp's attention also took a moment to return to the stage. "The woman. Oh, that woman! No longer from head to foot than from hip to hip: she is spherical, like a globe; I could find countries in her."

Shakespeare as Antipholus was, of course, performing his own jokes, and he found himself quite clever indeed. "In what part of her body stands Ireland?"

"Marry, in her buttocks: I found it out by the bogs."

While the audience was enjoying the cheap shot at Ireland, Bentley appeared in another window, again demanding payment, this time successfully. He also took a swig from an offered bottle.

Shakespeare continued his riff. "Where's Scotland?"

Kemp leered at the audience to heighten their expectation of another joke. "I found it by the barrenness;" and he explained by pinching an imaginary penny, "hard in the palm of the hand."

Bentley appeared in yet one more window, again stealing the show. This time Bentley was up against a huge man and his blowzy wife. Bentley made his demand, and the man rose from his perch at the window to loom over Bentley.

Shakespeare, meanwhile, sailed on with his geography puns. "Where stood Belgia, the Netherlands?"

Kemp appeared shocked at the mention of the country. "Oh sir, I did not look so low."

Nor did the audience as Bentley reached toward the huge man's blouse. This turned out to be a strategic error. The man locked his hands around Bentley's vest, raised him up, dragged him through the window, and dropped him into a rain barrel not too far below.

Judging by the audience reaction, Shakespeare should have considered incorporating this bit of business into the show.

Twenty-Five — Apothecary Surveillance

*T*he six *Pembroke's Men* wagons, resplendent in their yet untarnished green and gold, roared down the road, creating a dust cloud that, for those unlucky enough to rate the final coach, obliterated the fine summer view.

In the lead carriage Elinor rode with Shakespeare, Bentley and Burbage.

A small roadside marker came into view. Bentley leaned out of the coach to read it, and turned to the group to announce, "Northampton. Three miles."

A few hours later, Shakespeare and Elinor might have presented the very portrait of a young couple in love, but she was wearing her doctor's mask, robes and carried a black satchel. They sat on a bench opposite the apothecary shop. And waited.

Shakespeare was puzzled. "We are waiting for what to happen?"

"I hope nothing."

His question was answered by the urgent sound of running feet, as a distraught woman rushed down the road and into the shop.

Elinor rose. "There it is."

She told Shakespeare to follow her and went into the shop to eavesdrop. The woman could barely catch her breath. "And came down with the fever. And I can't tell if he hears me. Thrashing about…"

The apothecary reached, without needing to look, for a dark brown bottle of liquid, stopped with a cork and sealed with wax. "Give him this every once in a while. And seal up the windows and doors as best you can. Keep the children away."

The woman flew out of the shop, and Elinor followed her, trailed by Shakespeare. Up a couple of dusty alleys they finally came upon the woman's house, a small thatched-roof hutch with chickens and children scrabbling in the dust outside.

Elinor trailed the woman inside, indicating to Will to keep out. The woman was startled to find Elinor following her and frightened at her appearance.

"Are ye the Reaper?"

"No, I'm a doctor. May I have a look at him?"

The woman was already grieving. "He's dying, isn't he? He's got it."

Elinor checked the patient's extremities, felt for a pulse at each of his ankles, sensed his fever. She handed the woman a packet.

"Give him these several times a day. They may help with the fever. Keep the children away."

"Even at night?"

"Have them stay away. When did he get sick?"

"Seems Wednesday he wasn't himself."

"Have you a stall in the market?"

"We sell millet by the sack."

"Many rats of late?"

"Same as always. They take their portion."

Elinor led Shakespeare to the market, where he obediently followed her around, shouldering her satchel. She peered under the stalls, looking for rats, and examined the faces of the proprietors and buyers as they traded. She especially looked at hands, trying to distinguish dirt and bruises from the tell-tale blackened joints and digits.

As she worked, she explained to Will what she knew so far. "It has been believed for centuries that the plague is spread by bad air that moves from the far east — Italy and beyond — across the continent. And there may be some truth in that."

Shakespeare offered the common name. "The miasma."

"Yes. And history shows that this has happened before. Over the centuries, and the devastation has always come from the east, so it seems."

Will offered, "But you think it's not about the air."

Elinor shook her head in a single side-to-side shake, brushing away centuries of ignorance. "The plague is something on the rats. The ships bring eastern rats wherever trade takes them. The black death always begins in the port cities and spreads inland from there. I have seen this in Genoa, Hamburg, Antwerp, and now London."

She shook her head. "I didn't think it would spread to the inland market towns so fast."

Later, as the sun set, they were walking silently, each content to be in their own thoughts for a moment. They had found a meadow alongside a brook. Elinor took off her hot mask and shook out her dark tresses. Shakespeare noticed the key around her neck.

"Not English. Too grand."

She saw where he was looking. "Spanish. My great-grandparents fled to Italy."

Shakespeare was intrigued, as a botanist might be when first engaging in a first encounter with a species he had only previously seen in etchings. "You are a Jew?"

Elinor offered the only logical response. "There are no Jews in England. We are currently banished."

"We?"

"They."

"Makes sense. This key, then, is to your house?"

"In Toledo. We, they, will return someday."

"And in the meantime, you wander amongst the Christians." He considered that for a moment. "What you must think."

She kept those thoughts to herself and banished them with a knowing smile.

He was fascinated at his exotic find. "My deck has been shuffled. All is new."

Twenty-Six — The Smallest Cloud

The company was in the late steps of breaking down the stage. The teams of horses stamped impatiently, ready to roll the wagons out. Ben Bentley stopped directing the activities to handle an interruption.

"Mr. Bentley, sir?"

Bentley imperiously responded to the innkeeper as if to a worm. "Sir?"

The innkeeper remained cheerful. "And how will you be handling your account?"

"In the customary way, my man. The Earl of Pembroke will settle these accounts upon presentation."

"Unfortunately I do not know the gentlemen in question."

Bentley took offense. "He is not a 'gentleman in question.' He is the Right Honorable Earl of Pembroke, as honored by Her Majesty."

The innkeeper had seen it all before. "I don't mean to demean the Right Honorable Earl. I merely require assurance I will be paid."

As he headed toward the wagons with Elinor, Shakespeare caught the drift of the conversation and was cautiously alarmed. Would the company be broken apart in this hamlet far distant from London?

"You crinkle your right eye ever just so when you're worried," said Elinor.

"Hmmm. I did not know that about myself."

Elinor was in a playful mood. "When you are looking at yourself in a glass someday, I will tell you something to concern you. And you will see what I mean."

Shakespeare raised a finger to his lips as he strained to hear how Bentley was faring.

The innkeeper remained calm. "I've rounded it to six pounds seven. And your horses will be well cared for until we've settled."

Beaten, Bentley fished his purse from under his shirt and counted out the coins.

Twenty-Seven — A Fairy Dies in the Forest

As the company settled in at the Leicester Inn, Elinor was there, torn between following rumors of spreading death, and her delight in the effervescent Will, so full of life. To the company she provided a much-appreciated service: She comprised an audience of one during the development of this strange work they were struggling with under the working title of "A Summer's Romance" as Shakespeare tried to convey what he imagined and hoped he had written, to the players.

At the moment, he was working with Kemp, who was developing Bottom. "Will, you sit crosslegged here. Titania… that would be you, Lawrence… you are doting on him."

Lawrence Blue batted his eyes.

"Lovely, Titania. And maybe you could fall to your knees mid-speech…"

Lawrence, waving an ordinary stick filling in as a wand, had not yet figured out what Shakespeare had in mind for Titania, so he attempted a decidedly 'poetic' speech. Flutey, high and trilling.

"Be kind and courteous to this gentleman. Hop in his walks, and gambol in his eyes. Feed him with apricots and blueberries…"

Shakespeare cut him off. "Actually, that's 'dewberries' if it's not too much trouble…"

"Not at all." He dropped to his knees, as Shakespeare had suggested. "And dewberries, With purple grapes… and so forth."

Shakespeare pushed ahead. "Very nice. Now let's skip to 'do him courtesies.'The four of you…"indicating the four younger boys, "dance and twirl about him."

Lawrence waved his wand. "Nod to him, elves, and do him courtesies."

The four younger boys, whirled counterclockwise around Kemp with a long scarf held above their heads, With every few turns they crouched to their knees so that the circle of scarf appeared to not only circle, but dip from side to side.

Eleanor was delighted with the effect and burst into applause. "That is just splendid, boys."

The first Fairy called out, "Hail, mortal."

Shakespeare gave them their cue. "There you go — everyone join in!"

The four fairies cried out, "Hail!"

Shakespeare cued Kemp. "And then Bottom."

"I cry your worships' mercy, heartily. I beseech your worships' name."

"Cobweb," sung out one of the fairies.

Kemp continued. "I shall desire you of more acquaintance, good Master Cobweb. If I cut my finger, I shall make bold with you…." He interrupted himself to ask Shakespeare what in the world that meant.

"That means if he happens to cut his finger, he's going to make himself blood brothers with Cobweb."

Kemp was bemused by Shakespeare's bizarre intelligence. "How in the world did you come to know this?"

Meanwhile, the fairies kept their whirling.

"Oh Kemp, everyone knows if you cut yourself you can be blood brothers with someone."

Kemp looked skeptical. "Hmmff. New to me." He went back to script, "Your name, honest gentleman?"

Billy Judd, the second fairy, was by now quite dizzy. "Peaaaseblossoommm…"

The others, especially the young boys, laughed heartily with professional appreciation as Billy demonstrated a fairylike swoon.

But he wasn't being funny. He had fainted, out cold. Shakespeare ran to him and in a moment, Elinor was there, checking his joints, looking for breath.

"He is not well. We need to get him inside. His own room. Carry him in a blanket, and everyone keep your distance."

Later that night Shakespeare sat in a corner, his candle the only light in the room. He was writing, hearing entire dialogue exchanges in his head, playing them over again and again. And only then, when he had worked something out to his satisfaction, did he actually put quill to paper.

If one only saw this final part of his work, the actual putting words on paper, one would think he was writing like the wind. But that wasn't how it was.

Elinor sat near the sleeping Billy, who occasionally cried out from a deep sleep. She watched Will, and when his quill came to rest, she approached him.

"This is the first touch of plague on your company. You know it might be devastating."

"I am thinking that as well. What can we do?"

"Stop sharing. Stop sharing food. And handshakes. And even beds. Everyone needs to isolate themselves as much as they can."

Shakespeare only heard part of this. "Beds?"

"Not us. If I am going to die I want to die in your arms."

"I would prefer to live in yours."

Billy was choking. Elinor went to him immediately, but the choking continued, turning into a soft cracking sound.

"He can't get air."

She tried to work his throat open, but there was nothing she could do. She held his hand as his little life drifted away.

Twenty-Eight — Among the Angels

The small body in a winding sheet was lowered into the fresh grave, as Elinor and the entire Pembroke's Men company watched. All had been fond and protective of Billy and each of the survivors was wounded in their own way.

Shakespeare had been selected to say something, and as was his way, he had carefully crafted his thoughts, and revised and refined them, without putting a word on paper. When he gave his remarks, he spoke to each member of the company, locked eyes for a moment, and then moved to the next, speaking to each one, and ultimately, for each one.

"Here is our actor, all spirit, now melted into air, into thin air: And, like the baseless fabric of our diverse visions: the cloud-capp'd towers, the gorgeous palaces, the solemn temples, the great globe itself, yea, all which it inherit, shall dissolve and, like this insubstantial pageant faded, leave not a rack behind. We are such stuff as dreams are made on, and our little life is rounded with a sleep."

Shakespeare took a fistful of dirt in his hand, and released it over the sheet-wound body. All the company followed, paying their respects, each in their own way. Some with a handful of dirt, some with a nod, some with a spoken farewell. And then they were gone.

Lingering in the cemetery, Elinor and Shakespeare walked about, reading the gravestones, admiring the occasional stone angel.

"Here's a fine one! Any plumper and he'd be in danger of being taken and roasted for a squab."

"You will hurt his feelings."

They settled on the ground under the stone angel, making a pensive threesome.

Elinor was thinking about Shakespeare's farewell to Billy. "It's a wonderful gift that you can say what's in all of our hearts."

"Hmmm."

"Or maybe you say things that we hope are in our hearts and when you say them then we find out that they were there."

Shakespeare seemed to like that a little bit more and offered Elinor a slightly more interested, "HMMmm.!"

Elinor was still trying to get it right. "Or maybe, it's that we want to hear them said…"

It was becoming too much for him. He interrupted. "Buzz!?

Elinor feared she had insulted him. "Buzz?"

"Too much! It's all an act."

"What is?"

"Everything I say. A funeral oration. It's acting."

Elinor couldn't choose to believe whether he was telling the truth or if this was a way of pushing his emotions away. "You don't mean it when you say those things that are so beautiful to everyone?"

"Of course I mean it. But I can also see myself saying it. I am beside myself, judging."

Elinor tried to see it. "Two beings at once?"

"At the least. Me speaking, me thinking about my words wondering if I might refine them further, me watching others watch me, me watching myself, me seeing us in bed at night and wondering about what we'll be doing if we ever get back to London. All at once."

Elinor had visited asylums in her training. Mad people chained to their beds. People who switched from persona to persona, unsure which was the real self. "Might this be an illness?"

Shakespeare did not attempt to lessen her fears. He wasn't mad, but he could see things about himself that no one had expressed before. "Oh yes. A terrible affliction."

Elinor nor longer felt she was the doctor here. "Is there a cure?"

"I fear not."

"A fever is the cause?"

Shakespeare shook his head. "I think not. Rather, life itself."

He thought about it further. Surely he couldn't be the only one. "I'd wager you're the same."

Elinor could not imagine being the multi-conscious person he had described. She always knew who she was and what she was doing, one awareness at a time. "I think not. I am one person. I am here…" she put her hand over her breast, "…in my heart."

Shakespeare tried to explain. "If I touch your heart…" and he put his hand over her hand on her breast, "…and if I do this:"

He kissed her, a deep and passionate kiss, meant to take her breath away.

"And if I ask you what were you thinking just now, you would say…?"

Elinor gave it her best clinical reasoning, which was generally of a very high order. "I would say I was not thinking, but that I was being kissed."

"And that is all?"

"All."

"I must do better…"

He kissed her again, trying terribly hard to be persuasive. While kissing her, he opened his eyes to observe her and raised his eyebrows as if to ask, 'So?'

Elinor opened her eyes for a moment and saw him observing her, and she broke out laughing. And then she stopped laughing and tried to explain. "I am just Elinor. At this moment not a doctor, not a Jew. Just Elinor, being kissed by William. That is all, and that is enough."

Shakespeare smiled an enigmatic smile. What lay between them in understanding was the gap he needed to bridge.

Twenty-Nine — Talent Scouts

*T*he company was once more on the move, heading north in the heat of a blazing summer day. The green wagons still gleamed, and the horses shone. Yet there were signs that the company had made adjustments to life on the road, revelations that the romance had become slightly tarnished. The fabulous tassels that adorned the horses were now stowed, only brought out at the last possible moment before entering a town. Laundry was hanging out to dry wherever it could be fastened high enough above the dust. Skins of water and wine swung from the window ties.

The lead teamster saw a marker go by and called out, "Darby Town, two miles!" The call was repeated from wagon to wagon. Napping actors were roused, and laundry was gathered in.

Upon arrival in Darby Town, the company sent word around that there would be auditions, and that the lucky winner would have a chance to appear with the great Pembroke's Men Company of London. If all went exceedingly well, that young man might even be invited to join the Company and return with them to London and a possible career on the stage.

By noon, dozens of young boy applicants had gathered in the market. Each of the candidates were dressed in their mother's or sister's finest outfits. Many were wigged, and some were even rouged.

A colorful jousting tent had been set up to provide shade for Kemp, Burbage and Shakespeare who sat together as judges. A lutenist sat close by, ready to provide accompaniment when needed.

The first boy was in the midst of his audition, clearly dragged there by his mother,

His mouth was moving but unless you could read lips, what he might be saying was a mystery.

Burbage cupped his ear to make the point. "Can you bring that out a bit?"

The boy took a deep breath and turned a brighter shade of red. The result was a slightly audible sound. "Demetree us loves your fair. O happy fair!"

Someone on the committee said "Next," and the next boy stood before them.

"Your eyes are lodestars, and your tongues a sweet air. More tunable than lark to shepherd's ear."

Kemp observed to Shakespeare, "Or maybe more tunable than bark to shepherd's flark?"

Shakespeare brushed him off. "I think not."

A third boy was trying to make sense of his lines, "When wheat is green, when hawthorn buds appear. Sickness is catching: O, were favour so…"

Shakespeare attempted to see if the boy could take some direction. "Excuse me, when you say those words I don't understand them. Can you show us how sickness might be catching?"

The boy clutched his throat so tightly his faced turned pale. "Sickness, " he coughed quite convincingly, several times, "is catching: O, were favor so."

Shakespeare nodded in appreciation. "Thank you, Sir. Better!"

Without realizing it, Shakespeare had paid the boy the greatest compliment of his life. The boy wondered whether the word could actually have been meant for him. "Sir?"

"Of course. Even when you are only making an audition, you are already considered a gentleman of the theatre. Hence, 'sir.'"

"Thank you! Ever so much." The boy thought a moment longer. "Sir."

Shakespeare turned to his colleagues. "I rather like him."

The next boy was wearing pigtails that reached down to his waist. With his huge blue saucer eyes, he was quite stunning, for a boy or girl. He began to read. "My tongue's sweet melody. Were the world mine, Demetrius being bated,"

Shakespeare liked him and interrupted. "That's good, Can you improvise a song on it?"

The lutenist strummed a few chords and the pigtailed boy sang a beautiful improvised melody. "My tongue should catch your tongue's sweet melody…"

Burbage was quite taken. "Oh, that's lovely. Absolutely marvelous. And your name is?"

"Jonathan Little, sir."

"Have you a parent about?"

And with young master Jonathan Little aboard, the Company headed ever farther north, to Sheffield.

Thirty — Creating The Sheffield Man

*C*old rain had started with the dawn, and the clouds were heavy and low enough to obscure the higher glories of the Sheffield church. Elinor had made her visit to the apothecary, making inquiries as to the current maladies of the citizenry. Finding nothing alarming, she returned to the inn, and hearing familiar voices coming from the stables, she slipped inside to observe the Company at work.

Elinor could see at a glance that Shakespeare was oddly more intense than ever despite his evident calm. When he was worked up, he showed the opposite of what he was feeling. When others might pace, he was still to the extreme. When others might flash their eyes, he appeared to be almost asleep, turning inward. Elinor knew that he was at the precipice of frenzy, since he was lying flat on his back on the stable floor, eyes closed. The players walked around and over him, as if he was a fallen tree.

The fallen tree spoke. "Let's start with the moment where the mechanicals are rehearsing the Ninny's Wood scene. Flute?"

Flute was in Burbage's capable hands. As a great tragedian, his Flute's way of playing Queen Thisbe was to make certain his resonant voice would thrill an audience member asleep in the last row of the house.

"This is old Ninny's tomb. Where is my love?"

The character Snug was the lion. He came up behind Flute and gave a great, thrilling, roar. Thisbe appeared to be terrified by throwing up her hands a number of times and shrieking, finally dropping her mantle. Snug picked it up and shook it mightily.

Kemp, as Bottom playing Pyramus, walked into the scene, deliberately tripping over Shakespeare, and reacting to the lion. Kemp was also in larger-than-life heroic form.

"O, wherefor, Nature, didst thou lions frame? Since lion vile hath here deflowered my dear…"

Shakespeare interrupted without opening an eye. "Can you jump ahead to killing yourself?"

Kemp didn't bat an eye. "Not a problem." He switched back into character. "Out, sword, and wound the pap of Pyramus; Ay that left pap, Where heart doth hop." Here, Kemp stabbed himself as any great actor might, with both hands holding the dagger, and then staggering about for awhile. "Thus I die, thus, thus, thus…"

Shakespeare sat and then stood in an amazingly fluid motion, as if rising from the dead. "Can we stop it here for a moment?"

Kemp removed the dagger from his breast and declared, "I am stopped."

The actors gathered to hear what Shakespeare thoughts.

"Can I suggest we try a different notion here?"

They waited, and he continued after a moment.

"This little play within our play is being put on by actual everyday people, not Pembroke's Men, the great road company from London. Yet, when I hear us, I hear great men trying to be lesser people. We are condescending."

Burbage had a hard time with this. "Your worship, sir, we are great men from London and we are playing these mechanicals as idiots because they generally are, and that is intended to bring forth laughter."

Shakespeare neither agreed nor disagreed. "There are many ways to bring forth laughter. At our least, we can also deploy clowns and jugglers. But that is not our work here. There is more in them, and if we can find it and show it, we will have something new here."

Kemp was puzzled. "I confess, I do not understand."

Shakespeare tried to explain. "Normally, we are great men of the theatre playing great men of the world." He grabbed a poker lying nearby and held it up as if it were a sword. "We customarily act as if we each have one of these up our backsides, instead of a spine. I say, take the pokers out of your arses. It's not the exalted Ben Jonson or Kit Marlowe we're doing here — it's just plain old Will Shakespeare, and we're doing it for those faces at the skirts of our stage."

The actors were puzzling this through, feeling uncomfortable. Shakespeare continued. "Let's simply show them that our Jacks and Jills are just like themselves and see if that gets to their hearts."

Kemp was willing, but not sure. "I can try."

"Good. Then let's take a different approach to the rehearsal. You, Bottom, want to fix anything and everything Peter Quince suggests. So when Quince describes the lion, you have a better idea."

Kemp took a deep breath, and tried to become a new Bottom. "Masters!"

Shakespeare jumped in. "Look at them, bring them closer, talk to them as if you were brothers, or conspirators. Search their eyes and see if they are with you."

Kemp started again, putting his arms around the closest players and drawing them together. This time, instead of his stentorian theatre voice, he spoke as a real person might speak, one to the other. For a moment, it seemed as if he had completely gone off his lines. But in fact, he was staying with the script.

The difference transformed the others. With Kemp leading, they found their humanity.

"Masters! You ought to consider that a lion among the ladies is a most dreadful thing. For there is not a more fearful wildfowl than your lion living, and we ought to look to 't."

Snout agreed. "Therefore a prologue must tell he is not a lion."

Elinor put down her notebook. Something had caught her ear. The players had melted away and real people seemed to be talking. It was almost frightening. Had they lost themselves?

Kemp continued. "Nay. You must name his name, and half his face must be seen through the lion's neck, and he must say directly, 'Ladies…'"

Shakespeare was pleased. "Much better. I began to believe you. Now let's try to do that when the Queen of the Fairies wakes up with the magic juice on her eyelids and spies our Mr. Kemp for the first time. Kemp — can you look less handsome for our sake?"

Kemp made a funny face. "I'll do my best."

Lawrence Blue, once again, was Titania. "What angel wakes me from my flow'ry bed?"

Kemp began to sing, "The finch, the sparrow and the lark. The plainsong cuckoo gray…"

Lawrence fluttered his eyes at Kemp, "Gentle mortal, sing again."

But Shakespeare wasn't happy. He got up and looked right through Kemp and Blue, seeing something that he imagined, but that wasn't yet there. Suddenly he went over to Elinor and grabbed her death mask, and with her protesting, brought it over to Kemp.

"Put it on!"

Kemp thought he was joking. "What in the world?"

"Let's just say that Puck has, in his mischief, put a mask on Bottom."

"A doctor's mask?"

"No. We'll use something else — like a donkey. Put this on for now!"

Shakespeare waited and then turned to Lawrence Blue. "There, Titania, see if you can make us believe you are in love with this!"

Lawrence was a great young actor. He looked at the mask, and fell in love. "I pray these, gentle mortal, sing again. Mine ear is much enamored of thy note, so is mine eye enthralled to thy shape. And so on and so on." He was selling it. He simply burst out, "I love thee."

Shakespeare said simply, "This is good."

Kemp continued. "Methinks, mistress, you should have little reason for that."

Shakespeare spoke over him, "Better. Now stop 'acting' altogether."

Kemp was the first to make the leap into a real multi-dimensioned Shakespearian character. His Bottom now became the scaffold-builder, Niles.

Kemp inhabited the wisest donkey there ever was. "And yet, to say the truth, reason and love keep little company together nowadays. The more the pity that some honest neighbors will not make them friends."

Lawrence embraced the mask. "Thou are as wise as thou art beautiful."

And then there was silence. Kemp in his mask and Blue seemed for an instant to have actually fallen in love, staring deeply into each other's eyes.

Shakespeare gave it his benediction. "Beautifully played."

Thirty-One — A Letter Home

*T*he rain had not let up, and after the midday meal Elinor and Shakespeare had repaired to her room to make the most of the damp and dreary day. Now, with Will deeply committed to his nap, Elinor sat at a table near the only window where she could watch Will and, as a way of working through her thoughts, write a letter to her father.

She was describing the morning's rehearsal and Shakespeare's struggle to find something with his actors that did not yet have a name.

"At that moment, everything changed. If that boy, playing the Queen of the Fairies, could make us see what he saw when he looked into that terrible mask and discovered the humanity within — and be in love with it — then we could all begin to see there might be masks everywhere, preventing us from seeing each other as we are.

"And I wondered why there might be masks everywhere. Masks we hide behind. Maybe even obscurations we put up so as not to see what is in front of us.

"And then I remembered something you said from the Talmud, where Rabbi Ilai says we can see past the masks of a man by looking at his cup, his capital and his choler. I mentioned that to Will and he wanted to know what the Talmud was and how he could read it.

"And then he said that maybe we are all players acting our parts, hiding behind masks. At first I disagreed, wanting to test that idea through argument, but as I thought it through, I began to wonder. I thought about the pious person who is not always pious, but whose mask presents the same face always, whether so or not. I thought of the obedient face of the wife who doesn't know how she became a servant to her husband. Even the mask of a queen who knows that under her crown is just a little girl who grew up and is now expected to be always correct, even when she can't imagine the consequences when she takes her country to war.

"And finally, Father, I thought about my mask. Playing the role of the lover of the poet, traipsing around the countryside on a magical summer's journey, and ignoring what has been getting clearer to me by the day, that we are the miasma."

Thirty-Two — Bestseller

*T*he bookseller in Sheffield market was busy trying to tie his flapping canvas to a pole, hoping to keep his books dry while allowing customers to peruse his wares. Shakespeare and Elinor poked under the flap and wondered whether they might take a look 'round.

The bookseller quickly sized them up, going after his apparently easy mark first. "Madam, all the latest romances are right over here. Including our most popular…"

Elinor gently cut him off. "I am interested in the medical, actually."

"Aha! Household nostrums? Cure for the Black Death? Itchy feet? Right over here…"

Elinor moved in that direction somewhat skeptically, while the bookseller next descended on Shakespeare.

"And you, sir? What entertainments would please you today?"

"Anything on Venus or Adonis would do."

The bookseller was immediately suspicious. Was he being played with? "Venus or Adonis?"

"To be precise."

"How about Venus and Adonis?"

Shakespeare cocked a skeptical eye at the bookseller. "Oh? Is there such a thing?"

The bookseller eyed him as if he surely had come from a distant star.

"Venus and Adonis is our most popular book."

Shakespeare, of course, was absolutely thrilled, but kept that to himself. He glanced to see if Elinor had heard, but she was deep in browsing her medical texts.

"Really?"

The bookseller nodded proudly. "Cannot keep it in the stall."

"Oh. Do you presently have a copy?"

"Indeed. The fourth printing has just arrived." And he handed a copy to Shakespeare.

Shakespeare held the little volume. "Fourth? How remarkable."

The bookseller gave him a sly look. "They say it is hidden beneath many a pillow."

"Oh?"

The bookseller made a gesture toward his own waist to indicate it had a lot of sex in it. "You know?"

Shakespeare felt the time had come for the big reveal. "Actually, I do." He pointed to the name on the cover. "He, is me."

Whatever Shakespeare was saying was beyond the ability of the bookseller to understand. He read the name out loud. "Shack-speare."

Shakespeare nodded. "The same." And then he suddenly had an inspiration. "Would you like me to write my name in your copies? Your customers might like that."

The bookseller was disdainful, as if being offered rotten fruit. "I do not think they would want their copies so despoiled."

"Just a thought. How about if I sign one, and if it isn't sold by the time we leave tomorrow, I will buy it from you myself. Upon my honor."

The bookseller was very skeptical, but felt badgered. "Well. All right, then."

So Shakespeare signed one copy of Venus and Adonis, creating the first signed edition of anything. He did not have to buy it back.

Thirty-Three — The Parting

Shakespeare and Elinor backed out of the bookstall and into the mist. They caught sight of one of the Company's green wagons. As they drew nearer, they could hear Ben Bentley in a deal-making mode, whining about the high cost of provisions, denigrating the quality of the foods being offered, suggesting he'd be back for more if the price was right.

As the couple slipped past to avoid interrupting Mr. Bentley's negotiations, they could see that the wagon was already loaded with barrels of not particularly lovely food that had attracted a sizable population of rats. "The Company is like a ship," Elinor mused, "going from port to port."

"Are you looking for a figure of speech?"

"No. I'm looking at the spread of disease. As ships worked their way from east to west, the Death started at the ports where the ships first landed, and then the illness spread inland. Italy was first, then the southern coast of France, around to Spain, north to England. I am certain Sweden will be next."

"And the Company?"

"The Company moves from town to town. We have most likely been spreading the plague northward from London."

"That is a serious thought. I thought we were merchants of joy."

"I am afraid we have been carriers of disease. The only way for me to know is to go back and retrace our path and see what has taken place in our wake."

They walked on in the rain, which now matched their mood.

"What can we do, not knowing whether we are agents of illness?"

"Ideally, you should stay here, or return to London."

"But we have just begun to earn our way, and London has nothing for us, as far as I have heard."

"If you continue you may be spreading the disease. I cannot be part of it."

"We cannot stay, and we cannot go."

"At least get the rats out of the wagons. Don't let them go with you."

"They are nested in everything. The seats, the trunks."

"Burn them out, then."

"That is not possible. But I will see what we can do."

They trudged on toward the Sheffield Manor. Shakespeare looked at Elinor, the rain misting on her lovely forehead. "When will I see this countenance again?"

She didn't know, but saying so would make it worse, even final. "Maybe this was our hour."

Shakespeare tried to understand how his feelings in that moment, his heart-stopping sense of loss, fit in to his evolving human schema. He knew he had the power to see his choices and act. And he dismissed the wretched notion that somehow fate had dealt him this bitter moment and that he was powerless in its grip.

"When all is lost, we still can hold our aspirations. I will have that."

What he hadn't yet realized was that the first manifestation of helplessness was anger.

Thirty-Four — The Cleansing

"Damn rats! Out! Out!"

Richard Burbage woke up from a dream, thinking he had heard young Will yelling not far away.

"Damn you wretched vermin!"

It was no dream. Burbage opened his shutters and looked out to the courtyard below. Will Shakespeare had apparently gone mad and was tearing the stuffing out of the seats of one of their coaches.

"Will. Have you lost your mind? It is the middle of the night!"

Shakespeare paused and peered up into the gloom. "It is nearly dawn. Come down and lend me a hand."

Burbage pulled on a gown and rambled down the hallway, banging on most of the doors and proclaiming various versions of 'Will's gone mad and needs our help.'

Within a few minutes much of the Company had gathered to watch Shakespeare ransack the coach. Once in a while, as when he tore the covering off the stage coach door, a rat would escape, and Shakespeare would chase after it, yelling, "Damn you! Damn you!"

Shakespeare had ripped out the old hay that provided the stuffing for the wagon's upholstery. He struck a flint a few times, and soon he had an impressive fire roaring, dangerously close to the wagon.

Bentley was not happy to see his coach being ripped up. "Mr. Shakespeare. If I may inquire. What in the bloody hell are you doing?"

Shakespeare addressed the company. " As some of you know Elinor has left to retrace our steps, to see whether or not we have been carrying the plague from town to town."

Someone asked, reasonably, "And therefore you are tearing apart our transport?"

Shakespeare nodded. "Elinor strongly believed that certain rats are the messengers of the disease. Our rats began in London, and are likely to be those messengers. We can't, in all good conscience, do any less."

"You are mad, man. We will always have rats with us. They are in the food, in our trunks, in our draperies and costumes."

Shakespeare was adamant. "I will do this alone or I will do this with all hands. But if this is not done I will be leaving this company."

For a moment there was some silence as each contemplated what their future might look like without the young poet.

One of the young boys stood forward. "What can I do, sir?"

Shakespeare addressed him with deep respect. "You sir, can crawl into the dark spaces of this boot, find the nests, and rip them out."

"With pleasure, sir."

And before long, everyone had found a way to make a contribution. Every one of the carriages was disassembled to the greatest extent possible. The great draperies were opened up, hung over lines, and beaten clean. All costumes were carefully taken out, examined, and folded away.

As the dawn began to break, each rat that was found was chased away, or caught and strangled, which gave the youngest actors considerable pleasure. After several hours of labor, the entire company's goods had been stripped, cleaned and restored.

Shakespeare looked at one of the dust-covered youngsters and eyed the nearby mill stream.

The young actor could see what Will had in mind. He screamed. "No! I cannot swim!"

Shakespeare offered the consoling, "No time like the present to learn," chased the boy, caught him, and threw him into the stream. When he struggled and came to the surface, Shakespeare found another to catch. And before all the boys could be caught, one had a bright idea."

"Get Burbage!"

Burbage could do a pretty good impression of God when he needed to. "The first of ye who dares to touch this body will be drawn and quartered."

This frightened no one, and a healthy chase ensued, with Burbage being carried to water's edge and, with a few swings back and forth, finally tossed a goodly distance in.

Shakespeare, wishing to avoid the same fate, ripped off his own clothes and took a mighty dive into the gentle waters. And before long everyone, including Bentley, was in the stream, splashing around, and enjoying the all-too-rare morning bath.

They were, for the moment, the cleanest band of merry men in all of England. Shakespeare was pleased by what they had accomplished that morning. But he wished Elinor had been there to witness it.

Thirty-Five — A Lonely Journey

*E*linor's coach south was a ragged affair, stopping whenever anyone flagged it down, and the passengers who got on often got off in a few miles, leaving behind more dust and the occasional fistful of chicken feathers.

The slow progress gave Elinor time to try to bring some structure to her life after the assault that meeting Will had produced. First to put somewhere was the pain, the awful sense of loss, which now had once again replaced days of joy. She had her work, her research, her patients, her teaching. For so long this had meant so much, and she knew that soon the demands of her work would no doubt fill up her life once again.

In some way it was impossible for her to feel sadness that she might never see Will again. Simply knowing he existed had changed her feelings about the world. If someone like him was in it, then somehow all of humanity was quite a bit finer than she had recently believed. She might never see him, but he would still somewhere and that would please her.

Nonetheless there was, at the corner of one of her exquisite dark blue eyes, a tear, and it wasn't from the dust. She reached into a pocket and pulled out a long single white man's hose. She suddenly remembered that she was going to show off her human skin sewing skills by repairing a rip. She brought the orphaned garment to her nose, and breathed his scent in.

"Dusty ride, ain't it?"

The man who interrupted her thoughts was a workman sitting across from her, a bag of tools lying at his feet.

"Yes. Quite."

He was looking for conversation. "This is my first coach ride. At least one longer than a few hours. And you? Are you going all the way to London?"

"Possibly. I have some calls."

There were a few moments of silence, and then he explained why he was there. "They asked for me to come."

"Oh."

"Needed a boxmaker. I'm a carpenter, and they're shorthanded."

"Boxmaker?"

"Coffins. Baby boxes. Mama boxes. Daddy boxes. The Death has struck them hard."

Fearing the worst, she needed to know. "Where did you say you were headed?"

"Bedford Town."

Elinor took that in. And then she thought about the danger that lay ahead for the carpenter.

"You must take great care."

"Ay, know all about it. Keep the miasma out at night. Close up the windows."

"I don't think that will make a difference. I should explain. I am a doctor."

She could have told the carpenter she was a angel from the moon. He had no grasp of the notion that a woman could be a doctor.

So he explained to her how the plague worked. "You see, it comes at night with the bad air, and it gets into your skin. If you get water on your skin or wash in any way, you lose your protection and the miasma will get to you. I stopped washing when I they told me to come down."

Elinor thought about how she might get through. She thought that directness might work. "Is there anything I might say that you would believe — that I might know that could save your life?"

He smiled at her kindliness and sincerity. It was hard not to be touched. "I'm sorry, Missus Doctoress, but I already know what I need to know."

She refused to quit. "I'll tell you what. I am going to give you some information, and you can take heed or not. And here it is: the plague is carried by rats somehow. They don't get sick, but certain rats, if they live with or near you, will eventually kill many of the people nearby."

He gave her a smiling but essentially condescending look. "Well, thank you very much for that. Of course, I have been around the critters all my life, as everyone around me has too, and we're all pretty much alive until we die from something. And none yet has died from the Black Death. But thank you."

Thirty-Six — A New Disciple

*A*lthough it was mid-afternoon in Ripon Township, the low gray skies prevented even a hint that the sun might be up there, somewhere. But there was real light coming from the stage, as Shakespeare and his company had begun to understand the discipline of the new style, which began with Bottom and was now spreading to other living beings inhabiting other plays.

In the new style, stages, sets and costumes seemed to disappear as the reality of the human being began to show, real and unaffected. In a strange way, the artificial boundary between the lip of the stage and the audience just a few feet away had become less distinct, as if someone from the audience had just stepped up on the stage and begun to play a part, or as if an actor might easily slip into the audience and become a spectator.

That was one emerging revolution. The other was in the nature of the human beings Shakespeare was writing. They were beginning to show something that had never been seen before — an awareness of themselves as people capable of making choices, not on the theatrical stage, but the human stage.

A soft drizzle had begun. As usual, Shakespeare watched the audience closely from the stage. And today, something caught his eye. A richly-dressed younger gentleman was watching the play with great intensity, while two aides held a small purple shade of some sort, above him. The young man's mouth was slightly agape. And when Shakespeare spoke, he hung on every word and subtly imitated Shakespeare's body language.

Shakespeare was playing John of Gaunt, and was trying out a newly revised speech that regularly had the effect of getting the audience to shout 'Huzzah,' in spontaneous agreement. Shakespeare wanted to see how far he could move them.

"This royal throne of kings, this scepter'd isle, this earth of majesty, this seat of Mars…" Shakespeare moved toward the audience, sweeping them into his England with a broad and inclusive gesture, "This other Eden, demi-paradise, This fortress built by Nature for herself…"

At that moment, another player whispered to Burbage, who suddenly seemed alarmed at the news. Burbage coolly moved closer to Shakespeare, even though he was in mid-sentence.

"King of Scotland. Stage left. Don't look."

Shakespeare managed to continue, "Against infection and the hand of war, this happy breed of men, this little world…"

Shakespeare, being capable of being in his character's reality, while quite aware that he was also himself, realized that he was playing to the once and possibly future king, and spoke even more forcefully.

"Or as a moat defensive to a house, against the envy of less happier lands, This blessed plot, this earth, this realm, this England."

There was a hush among the audience at the conclusion of the speech, and finally one man, James VI, King of Scotland, clapped his gloves together. The audience had now become aware of royalty in their midst, and followed his lead, and soon the ovation was tremendous.

At the end of the play, the entire company gathered on stage and bowed low to the king — until he was heard to say, in a brogue so thick that only his dog could understand it, "Up, up, up. Rise up all of ye. Enough scraping and such."

Aided by his men, who were necessary to support the monarch at every step, King James, almost the same age as Shakespeare but withered by his infirmities, shuffled to the edge of the stage, where he beckoned the young Shakespeare to come to him.

Shakespeare leapt down from the stage and once more bowed deeply.

King James gestured for him to rise. "You are Shakespeare, and the poet of this marvel?"

"I am, your highness."

James gave him a conspiratorial look, managed to get his arm around Shakespeare, drew him close, and confided, "I am a writer, too."

Somehow, with James, the closer the proximity, the thicker the brogue. Shakespeare processed the unaccustomed accent and managed an appropriate look of surprise and delight. James gestured to one of his men who handed a slim volume to the king. James thrust the book toward Shakespeare, but didn't yet let go of it.

"From our recent witchcraft trials."

Shakespeare nodded. "I have heard of them."

James was modest. "I have scribbled the definitive account." He studied Shakespeare's face to make certain his next insight would register. "They are amongst us!"

"Indeed."

"And now I have shown how they may be discovered and tried."

"I will read it with the greatest of interest."

James barely heard him. "And how torture is the secret to revealing and testing them. I have devised the best."

James relinquished the book. What to do when a royal has presented you with such an unwanted gift? "I am honored," said Shakespeare.

They were interrupted by a tradesman carrying something for the king. The man was an armorer, and held a presentation box for the king's perusal.

"Your spurs, your highness."

James opened the box and held one up. "Oh, these are fine indeed."

He nodded, and the box was handed off to an aide. The steel maker made his bow and backed away.

"I come from Scotland to Sheffield for my steel," James explained to his new friend. "There are fine craftsmen here."

And then, he commanded to one of his men, "Clear our space!"

The audience was shooed away, and now Shakespeare stood alone with James, in the drizzly courtyard. James, true Scot that he was, hardly noticed the wet.

"I have heard of your Henry plays. I have had parts of them played for me. I was stirred. Quite stirred, in fact."

Shakespeare was genuinely touched. "Thank you, your highness."

James continued with his thought. "But until today, I have never seen the full possibilities of how a king might speak. When my parents died, I was too young. And then, not from my courtiers. Not from my tutors."

Astounded, Shakespeare simply looked up at the king.

"And until today, I have never heard what a king might say, if he were a great king. Now I have seen how I might be."

Thirty-Seven — The Stalker Catches Up

*I*n the course of a road company's summer, there is that one day where everything seems to have come together.

This was that day. Outside the entrance to the Ripon Inn's courtyard, the trumpets and drums of the Pembroke's Men made a joyful noise as the crowds pressed in from all sides. Vendors doled out their food as fast as they could ladle it. A maskmaker was handing his wares to the children, and toymakers peddled ratchety noisemakers. A bilboquet purveyor showed off his skills tossing and spearing the tethered wooden ball with his spindle, challenging the passersby to match him.

The company's own barker herded the crowd into the ticket line. "Come see the drama that brings kings to Sheffield! This is the one, and this is your last chance to be part of history! There's room for all! No pushing!"

He surveyed the huge crowd and observed to himself, "Unless it's too late, and then pushing won't help."

In the crowd a large family pressed forward, remarkable for a singular pale daughter whose reddish hair was a beacon amongst the drabber locals.

Ben Bentley stood at the entrance to the courtyard, selling tickets and stuffing his pockets with coins, looking as if he had been starved cruelly for too long and was now dangerously overeating.

Eventually the trumpeters and drummers marched from outside the theatre to the stage, where the company was ready to begin their current version of Richard II. With a final flourish, grand enough to have signaled a royal arrival, the musicians cleared the stage. For a moment there was a glorious silence, and Richard Burbage, dressed as Richard the King, took center stage and with great pleasure surveyed the huge and excited crowd.

He could not help but notice the redheaded girl. Had Bentley let in too many people to fit the space? It seemed as if they were holding each other up, packed so tightly that they seemed to sway together. And the girl — she was standing, but also, it seemed, asleep.

The huge banners waved and snapped in the breeze: lions rampant on a blue field seemed to spring and retreat.

"Now is the winter of our discontent Made glorious summer by this sun of York…" Burbage thrilled the crowd when he unveiled the pure pealing tenor of his upper voice, "and all the clouds that lour'd upon our house in the deep bosom of the ocean buried."

Something was wrong. The crowd was trying to pull away from a disturbance, but was constrained by the tight packing. The result was a human whirlpool as circles of people collapsed to their knees and others fell over them.

A voice called out, "Give room! Give room!"

As the whirlpool widened, revealed at the center was the redhaired girl, who lay on the ground.

There was a momentary pause in which things could have gone this way or that. The worst would have been if someone had called out, "Plague!.."

Which they did.

In the tumult that ensued, some people rushed the stage, sensing it might be a path of least resistance. The drapery that backed the stage was soon ripped and trampled, and before long the boards and trestles that made the stage itself were reduced to scrap.

Some of the crowd turned their anger on the company. "It is you who brought it to us!"

The actors were spat upon, shoved, some even stripped of their costly costumes. Some members of the troupe panicked, running away or attacking the crowd. Shakespeare had focused on guiding people to the inn doorways where they could safely find their way out. While he was helping a family, an older man walked up to Shakespeare and stared at him, almost crazily.

Finally, the man spoke. "It's not worth the bother."

Shakespeare didn't understand the intent. "What, precisely, is not worth it, my good man?"

"Anything. Anything." He wandered away and then came back to clarify his thought. "Nothing."

A few hours later the entire company gathered where the stage had so recently been standing.

Ben Bentley spoke. "There is no more money. We were deeply in the pit even before today, and now, it is much, much worse. I am ruined, basically."

Kemp's face burned bright red. "And what about us? Where are the promises from the Earl?"

Bentley would have looked shifty even if he had nothing to hide. When he did, in fact have something, his eyes narrowed even more, and his upper lip trembled. "I have been attempting to reach him, but messages have been spotty."

Burbage looked resigned to being shortchanged once again. Such was life in the arts. "What about our shares in the new theatre?"

Bentley feigned mystery and surprise. "What new theatre?"

Shakespeare's rage was barely controlled. "Allow me to quote you. Ben Bentley, May the Second, quote: 'And for each of you that completes the tour, the Earl has promised to build a new theatre on the banks of the Thames, and each of you will have owner's shares.' Unquote."

Bentley smiled at Shakespeare's naiveté at having taken him seriously. "The Earl seemed inclined at the time to come to such an agreement."

"But he had not?" Shakespeare rose from his barrel, right hand now reaching across his own belly. Was it just resting on his left hip?

"Agreement is a word with some flexibility." Bentley took a step backward.

Shakespeare moved on Bentley, as if to draw. "Piss on you and your deception!"

And with that, Ben Bentley ran off.

The company was beaten. Because he had risen to confront Bentley, Shakespeare was now the only one stand-ing. He remained standing and surveyed the others as he thought through their options.

"My friends! We have worked together well, and I am grateful for each and every one of you. For your efforts on the boards, for your friendship, and for your willingness to make yourselves part of my experiments."

Burbage responded for them all. "Hear, hear! And we're grateful for your plays, Will."

Shakespeare nodded thanks, and continued. "During the summer of our journey, fortune has smiled upon me."

No one knew what he meant. So he explained. "I can help fund our way back to London. We won't be posh, but we won't starve."

As the news sank in, there were grateful cheers.

"I ask only one favor. That we perform our new comedy to those who would brave this autumnal cold. Let us do it tonight, by the stars and whatever lights we may produce."

Thirty-Eight — A Starry Night's Dream

Now that the stage was gone, most of the props and costumes beyond repair, and even daylight itself no longer available, all that was left was the Company, playing in the middle of the inn's courtyard, surrounded by a small, rapt, audience, occasionally wetted by rain, illuminated by a few candles and lanterns, stars and the moon amongst the clouds, and a few persistent fireflies.

The new style of playing had permeated the Company. There was no orating, just characters speaking to each other and to the audience as good friends might.

Bottom and his players had their moment as Pyramus and Thisby, the lovers had magic worked upon them by the fairies, and finally all that the author's handiwork had undone was woven back together.

Shakespeare, as Oberon, gave his final farewell. "Trip away; make no stay. Meet me all by break of day."

He started to exit, but suddenly changed his mind and instead sat down among the audience. He glanced around, thought he saw Elinor, but on closer look, saw that it was not her.

Puck gave his final speech, one that was destined to bring an evening of magic to a close from that evening 'til the end of time.

"If we shadows have offended,
Think but this, and all is mended—
That you have but slumbered here
While these visions did appear.
And this weak and idle theme,
No more yielding but a dream,
Gentles, do not reprehend.
If you pardon, we will mend.
And, as I am an honest Puck,
If we have unearnèd luck
Now to 'scape the serpent's tongue,
We will make amends ere long.
Else the Puck a liar call.
So good night unto you all."

Puck was inspired in the moment and reached into the audience to those closest.

"Give me your hands if we be friends,
And Robin shall restore amends."

And instead of applause, for a moment, each member of the audience held hands with an actor or with each other, something that had never happened before in any play that any of them had performed or seen. Something had been bridged between the mirror and the mirrored.

Thirty-Nine — Slouching to London

The once gay red feather bridal plumes that adorned the horses' foreheads now drooped in the rain, as what was left of Pembroke's Men pulled out of Sheffield.

The mud tried to suck Will's foot in with every step, but he was determined to share the burden with the lead horses. Burbage, in sympathy with both Shakespeare and the horses, walked next to the other lead horse, enjoying slopping in the mud.

For a while they slogged on, bearing the punishment. Finally, Burbage found the bright side.

"A good run, nevertheless, Will."

Forty — Theatre on the Move

Six months later, Richard Burbage stood alone in the middle of a fine, timbered theatre. A clattering in the distance and some swearing closer by announced the arrival of William Shakespeare, brushing the snow off his coat.

"There you are! Happy Christmas, Will."

"And the same to you. Your message said the Lord Chamberlain's Men need a theatre. This is not it?"

Burbage shook his head. "No more. My father and I built this structure twenty years ago. And we own it, free and clear."

Shakespeare was unwilling to admit his puzzlement. "All good."

Burbage explained the minor detail. "Unfortunately, the man who owns the land will not renew our ground-lease."

"Not good."

"He wants to keep our building for his own purposes. He wants to steal it."

"Does he own the building?"

Burbage shook his head. "Our lease says it is ours to do with what we may."

Shakespeare lit up. "Then let us!"

Burbage gave Shakespeare a quizzical look.

Shakespeare explained. "I know a man."

One day and one night later, Peter Street led his team of workmen, including the newly formed acting company Lord Chamberlain's Men, to the base of the Shoreditch Theatre. As they dragged in ladders and bags of tools, Street gave his team the plan. "First, plaster comes off."

Six hours later, now the middle of the night, with plaster dust having turned the men into ghosts of themselves, the building had become a bare frame of timbers rising into the night. Peter gathered them once again.

"Then, we knock it out from the inside, and drag it away. Let's start at the top and work our way down. We're keeping this part, so go careful. We need two teams — one to pull the timbers down, and the other to drag them."

The men began to head off in their various directions when Peter called for their attention one more time. "And although you all can probably see this for yourselves, take care to not stand under the timbers when we're cutting them free."

The work resumed as the sun began to creep up in the east over the Thames. Some of the men hung precariously from the beams as they worked them loose. Others guided the timbers to the ground, where the drag teams worked like horses, pulling each beam to a barge that waited on the river.

As the dawn came into its own, red and gold, the team rode the barge, standing on the bones of their new theatre as they were towed across the Thames. Behind them was the mighty outline of Westminster. Ahead, the South Bank.

Shakespeare and Burbage were grimy and exhausted. Shakespeare summed it all up. "The theatre."

Burbage nodded, almost too exhausted to speak. "A filthy business, no question. I don't know why we persist."

Forty-One — She is Not at Home To You

Shakespeare rapped on Elinor's door and waited. After a few minutes, he knocked once more, and then, discouraged, turned to leave.

The door opened behind him. Avrahim peered into the dim hallway. "Yes?"

"Good day to you, sir. And you are Abraham?"

Avrahim was pretty clear who this might be. "And you are the poet?"

Shakespeare offered his hand. "Will. Has Elinor returned to London, then?"

They were close to each other, separated across the threshold. "She has, fortunately. Alive and well. But not living here."

"Oh?"

"She is in the employ of a wealthy family presently."

Shakespeare thought about what that could mean. What private family could afford their own physician? "No more rats?"

Avrahim chuckled. "There will always be rats."

Shakespeare nodded, unable to read Avrahim. "Please convey that I called."

Avrahim was embarrassed to be the bearer of what was to follow. "She instructed me that if you called, to say that she did not wish to see you."

Shakespeare nodded, hurt but not surprised. "I understand. Nevertheless, we are opening our new theater, the Globe, and you are both always welcome."

Avrahim said simply, "I will tell her."

"And please convey to her that I am no longer murdering England in the same old way. She will understand."

Avrahim couldn't help but sense there was a joke lurking there. "I am certain she will be pleased to hear that."

Forty-Two — The Threat

The splendid gold throne that Shakespeare had sat in many months ago when he and Marlowe were looking for props, now rocked from side to side in the bright sun as it sat in its drayage wagon, moving through London traffic.

Lord Salisbury, so extremely scoliotic that his resulting height was barely five feet and his breathing perpetually compromised by his twisted and compressed rib cage, arrived at the Globe theatre just in time to witness the throne appear. Salisbury peered upward with visible distaste at the spectacle of the rough men grappling with the near sacred seat as they brought it inside an unquestionably secular venue.

Workmen were everywhere, rushing to finish the theatre. On stage a rehearsal was in progress, with Burbage playing Richard II in a scene about succession that found him passing the crown to various applicants.

Salisbury and his men entered, and benches were brought so that they could seat themselves in the center of the courtyard, facing the stage.

A deliveryman approached Shakespeare on the stage. "Where would you have it?"

Shakespeare directed him to place the throne at the back of the stage, then leapt off the stage. He approached Lord Salisbury and greeted him with a careful bow, although it was impossible to bow low enough to actually appear to be subservient to the diminutive Salisbury. As a result, every encounter inherently began with Salisbury assuming he had been insulted.

"My Lord, welcome to the Globe."

Lord Salisbury let his displeasure be known. "I know that throne."

"The throne, M'lord?"

"Where did you come by it?"

Puzzled by Salisbury's focus on the throne, Shakespeare trod carefully.

"A theatrical supplier. I know not its provenance prior."

Salisbury was pleased to have discovered another source of leverage over this theatre and didn't mind disclosing it. "The Archbishop of Canterbury. From his chapel. I knew it well."

Shakespeare held up his hand to suspend the rehearsal, feeling it might somehow make things worse. But Salisbury overruled him.

"Let them continue. We are here to license, or withhold such, for your company and your theater. What is this work?"

"Richard the Second."

Lord Salisbury raised an eyebrow. "And the theme?"

"The divine right of kings."

Salisbury was interested. "For or against?"

Shakespeare turned and interrupted his actors. "Balm speech, please. And to the point, if you may."

Burbage understood, and provided an edit on the fly.

"So when this thief, this traitor, Bolingbroke,
Shall see us rising in our throne, the east,
His treasons will sit blushing in his face,
Not able to endure the sight of day,
But self-affrighted tremble at his sin.
Not all the water in the rough rude sea
Can wash the balm off from an anointed king;
The breath of worldly men cannot depose
The deputy elected by the Lord:
For every man that Bolingbroke hath press'd
To lift shrewd steel against our golden crown,
God for his Richard hath in heavenly pay
A glorious angel: then, if angels fight,
Weak men must fall, for heaven still guards the right."

Lord Salisbury was pleased with the speech, for what Royalist could quarrel with its philosophy? "I approve your sentiments, and will approve your continuing until and unless there is a new king."

Shakespeare was alarmed. "My Lord?"

"I believe it may be best to suspend theatre in London for a few years to give the new king a chance to restore the church in whatever direction pleases him."

Shakespeare sensed that a second plague was about to be visited upon them. "Suspend the theatre? Surely, such a suspension would be the death knell of our companies."

Salisbury did not find such a prospect to be a great concern. "That may be. As I do not yet speak for the new crown, I cannot say what he might say. But speaking for myself, I would suggest you and your men find an alternate means to provide yourselves with sustenance."

He looked around the Globe, imagining alternative uses. "This may serve well as a rendering facility, with the ability of these walls to contain stench. Good-day, gentlemen."

And with that, the entourage swept out of the building.

Burbage leapt off the stage and joined Shakespeare to assess the threat. "As long as Elizabeth reigns, we are safe."

And suddenly, Salisbury returned, whether having overheard, no one could tell. "I may have forgotten to mention. I hold the succession in my hands."

Shakespeare bowed. "There could be none more worthy, my Lord."

And Salisbury left once again.

Shakespeare continued with Burbage. "His cousin, Bacon, is close to James."

Burbage considered that. "And when the crown passes…"

Shakespeare completed his thought for him. "It may well be the Scot."

Shakespeare contemplated the prospect of King James of Scotland as king of England.

"We may only pray that he arrives here having left in Scotland that cast of mind that finds a suspect witch under every roof."

Forty-Three — Fairies on the Thames

*T*he opening of the Globe Theatre brought out what seemed like most of London. Even though only a small part of the crowd had any hope of actually getting inside, there was a great celebration going on which simply fed on itself. A brass ensemble played from risers. Jugglers, magicians, pickpockets, and food vendors all plied their trades. A banner draped high across the entrance proclaimed, 'A Midsummers Night's Dream.' Ticket vendors waited directly below.

And in front of the vendors were the scalpers. "Stalls, boxes, heaven. Last chance!"

Shakespeare, Burbage and the other shareholders of the Lord Chamberlain's Men stood discreetly to the side, observing the crowds.

Burbage was pleased. "An auspicious beginning. So many have come."

Shakespeare was wondering about the tomorrows. "And now — how to keep them coming?"

But that reverie did not last. Shakespeare saw Elinor in the middle of a swirl in the crowd and rushed toward her.

Standing close to each other, the chemistry between them was powerful. But something held them back.

Will spoke first. "I thought you were gone forever."

"I have been here only a short while."

"I went to your apartments."

"My father is there."

They gazed at one another, trying to discover what the other was feeling. They both spoke at once.

"I didn't know what to think."

"I thought you had stopped writing…"

And they stopped. There was pain for both of them.

Shakespeare needed to get dressed. "Can we meet later?"

"Of course."

Forty-Four — Embers

Judging by the spaciousness of his apartments, the completeness of the furnishings down to the fine brass tools that stood next to the handsome fireplace, Shakespeare had begun to prosper. The fire itself, though, barely supported a flame as he and Elinor entered the room.

Elinor broke what had not been the first long silence. "I have missed you. Every day I have missed you."

"I was afraid you were no longer in this world, and so I was beginning to love it less." And then he added, "Even though you hated me."

"I never hated you. I simply saw what was actually happening."

"Were you successful in Sweden?"

Elinor at first began to say, 'no,' but changed her mind. "If you mean, solved the black death, no. I was able to convince them to keep the rats from leaving the ships, and that seems to have slowed things."

"That is something."

Elinor brought it back to them. "And now I'm back."

One might have thought that Shakespeare would have been pleased. But he was troubled. "This is harder for me to accept than I had thought possible."

"Our summer…"

He finished her thought, "Was my paradise."

"And now?"

"The world is much with me. When the queen dies, theatre in London may also die. And then I will leave."

"The road to Stratford once again beckons."

"My family. My farm." He looked at her. "Elinor, I am in love with you and feel you in my heart with every pulse. I am in love with that love, and will carry it with joy to my grave."

"And I love you, Will. Then and now."

Shakespeare was filled with sorrow as he recognized his fears. "I am afraid to love you now. If I must leave London, I will needs carry not just one, but two lost Elinors in my heart. I fear it will be defeated by the burden."

He changed the subject. "Let me walk you home."

"You can help me find a cab."

The last flame in the embers flickered and was gone. A fine white ash covered the coals, but underneath, they were not yet cold.

Outside, in the gloomy night, Shakespeare found a cab and helped Elinor step up. They kissed briefly, a brush of lips, before the door closed. Shakespeare watched her looking back through the rear window as she disappeared into the mist.

Forty-Five — So, My Prince, What Will it Be?

On the south bank of the Thames, not far from the Globe, while a few boats with fisherman slowly drifted with the current, Shakespeare worked with Jonathan Little, whom Pembroke's Men discovered a few summers ago in Northampton.

Little was now in his young twenties, and had proven himself to be a fine young actor. He was working on a new role, his first as a male. His character's name was Hamlet, King of Denmark, and the play was still in development.

"…that dread of something after death. The undiscover'd country from whose bourn no traveler returns…"

Shakespeare lifted a single finger and Jonathan halted. "Can I make a suggestion? You seem to be thinking before you are speaking."

Jonathan thought about that and agreed. "I am. I am thinking that Hamlet is thinking about what it is he is about to say."

Shakespeare cast about for a way in. "Maybe you can't know it until you say it and hear it. It's a burst from your heart."

"All right. Sure." But he wasn't so sure.

Shakespeare explained a bit more. "You were not born to be a disturbed or tormented soul. You were born a prince, groomed to become the King of Denmark."

"To the manner born.'"

"Exactly. You have had the best tutors. You have been instructed in statecraft. You are ready to have trusted advisors. You are ready to be a strong leader."

Jonathan took this in, nodding, letting it in a little.

Shakespeare fed him some more. "And then. And then you learn that your uncle is probably the murderer of your father, and that your mother is now married to your uncle. To put a point upon it: your father's murderer is making the beast with two backs with your mother."

Little was wide-eyed. "Oh!"

Shakespeare was warmed up. "And that's not all, my prince. In this world, when your father is murdered, you must avenge his death. Not just that — when a king is murdered, you must avenge the nation."

Little was letting himself become Hamlet. "I will!"

And then Shakespeare crossed him. "Or will you? There is a prohibition against murder in our Christian world."

Little was suitably confused. "Yes. But…"

Shakespeare took it all the way. "And there is an even greater prohibition, if such a thing is possible, against the murder of a king. When you murder a monarch, you set the entire nation adrift. There is no greater crime than the murder of a monarch!"

Now Shakespeare was his full size, looming over young Jonathan. "So, my prince, what will it be? Avenge thy father and murder the country? What would a great prince do? Kill the king? Or given such an impossible choice — a choice that no man should have to make — kill himself?"

Jonathan had turned rather pale. Shakespeare nodded for him to begin again.

Jonathan was now genuinely torn, suffering the terrible choice. "To be, or not to be:…"

Shakespeare was molding on the fly. "Excuse me for interrupting again. There is one more thing."

"Yes?"

"Life is a gift. We are not queried, upon our birth, whether we prefer to accept this gift or refuse it."

Jonathan Little nodded in agreement. "Indeed…"

"Therefore, there comes a time in each life when we should become aware that we are unwitting beneficiaries of this gift. As if, upon birth, a fusty old aunt handed you a massive chest, gnarly and filthy from holding coal for a century or so, and given it to you. At some point in your life, you might suddenly wake up and say, 'Why am I dragging this chest around with me?' And you might answer, 'Because I like it,' or 'Because I can use it,' or 'Because I can clean it up and make it beautiful once again.' Or you can chuck it. But at some point, you can decide.

"For you, Hamlet, it is the same with the gift you have been given with your life."

Shakespeare indicated that Little was to begin again. "Now…"

And Jonathan Little began again as Hamlet, now torn by these terrible, unresolvable cross-currents, "To be, or not to be: that is the question: Whether 'tis nobler in the mind to suffer the slings and arrows of outrageous fortune, or to take arms against the sea of troubles, and by opposing, end them,"

Shakespeare said simply, "Thank you. I like that."

Burbage had been listening. Shakespeare asked him, "Richard, be Claudius for us, would you? 'Hamlet, where is Polonius?'"

Burbage complied. "Now, Hamlet, where's Polonius?"

Shakespeare queried Little in the moment, "Jonathan, what are you feeling toward the king?"

"Hatred. Bloody red rage."

"Good. Now try to hide it."

Burbage picked it up again. "Now, Hamlet, where's Polonius?"

Jonathan was daggers. "At supper."

"At supper! Where?"

Jonathan seemed mildly possessed, but made some kind of inner sense. "Not where he eats, but where he is eaten: a certain convocation of politic worms are eating at him."

Shakespeare jumped in. "More Northampton!" Which Jonathan understood to mean go closer to his home dialect. "And insultingly close!"

Jonathan moved in on Claudius. "Your worm is your only emperor for diet: we fat all creatures else to fat us, and we fat ourselves for maggots: your fat king and your lean beggar is but variable service, two dishes, but to one table: that's the end."

Burbage as Claudius, "Alas, alas!"

Jonathan raved on. Or was he raving at all? "A man may fish with the worm that hath eat of a king, and a cat of the fish that hath fed of that worm."

"What dost thou mean by this?"

"Nothing but to show you how a king may go a progress through the guts of a beggar."

Shakespeare felt something was missing. "I'm not sure it will play to the stalls. What is this king making progress through a beggar?"

Little makes it clear he understands. "The king is shite."

Shakespeare nods solemnly. "Excellent. Now convey that."

Now Jonathan conveys his disgust. "Nothing but to show you how a king may go a progress through the guts of a beggar."

Burbage can't remember what his lines were supposed to be, so just improvises along. "Fuck you, you whimpering little prince."

Jonathan joined him in jumping off the track. "And fuck you, Claudius."

Shakespeare intervenes. "Excellent, But we will keep our subtext to ourselves."

Burbage was pleased with the progress of young Jonathan. "This is coming along, Will. Your characters are becoming interesting people, the likes of which we have not seen on the boards before. This Hamlet, the way young Jonathan has him, even more than what you or I have been doing, is different."

Forty-Six — Elixir

The Company was gathered, every member, from the famous leading men to the younger boys who played both women and young men, to the strong hands who moved draperies and props.

It was a moment of drama, and Shakespeare intended to make his effect upon them.

"I have word that upon succession, this theatre, and all theatres in England will be shuttered for a time. Maybe a few years, maybe a decade or longer."

Shakespeare surveyed the Company as the news sunk in.

"A generation will live that remembers what the theatre was during the reign of Elizabeth, and then time will bring those who don't.

"Let us grieve not for that unknowable future. Let us celebrate what we have done. We have trod these boards, working them smooth with our pacing, our turns, our bended knees, our fallen villains and heroes. We have brought to life our Richard, our Henry, our Puck and our dear Bottom."

A voice called out, "Don't forget Hermia."

"I will not forget Hermia, nor will you."

Shakespeare took a moment to survey the wonderful theatre they had built with their own hands. "And then, in this sacred space, yet barely consecrated, another activity will come, possibly more useful to the next bearer of the crown: a slaughterhouse of animals, or of ideas, or even of souls.

"We will not know.

"If this comes to pass, grieve not. Bury your playbooks that the worms may weep and laugh. And finally, may we recall, as long as we are able, what we have done here together, working as a company, blessed by the alchemy of our chance mixing, distilling what we have brewed, intoxicating many by our magic, for so long as our elixirs retain their potency."

And then there was silence. The Company was in suspense.

Forty-Seven — To Comfort the Dying Monarch

*T*he Thames was eerily calm that night as the royal skiff brought Shakespeare to the dock. He was met by several courtiers, who made sure he stepped off without mishap. One of them looked Shakespeare up and down. "Haven't you forgotten something?"

"I assure you I have not."

"But you have no books, no papers."

"Rest assured."

Down one corridor and another, Shakespeare was led to the Queen's chambers.

The Queen appeared to be lying face down, but it was hard to tell since she was surrounded and given privacy by numerous maids, several of whom supported a drape.

A secretary spoke. "Your Majesty, Mr. Shakespeare is here."

Shakespeare was shown a stool near Elizabeth's head, and gestured to sit.

The Queen managed to turn her head so that she could see her friend.

Shakespeare slipped off his stool into a bow. "Your Majesty…"

"Mr. Shakespeare. They are bleeding me."

"May your humours be restored."

"Thank you for the unusual wishes. I was asked if there was anything I wanted while suffering so, and I asked for you."

"I am flattered."

Your voice pleases me. I would hear it."

"Reciting? What would please Her Majesty?"

"Did you bring a library?"

"I have, your Majesty."

"Then, the death of Arthur might cheer me up."

Shakespeare thought for a second or two, and then began.

"But ever King Arthur rode throughout the battle of Sir Mordred many times, and did full nobly as a noble king should, and at all times he fainted never; and Sir Mordred that day put him in devoir, and in great peril."

On the other side of the Queen, the maids had pulled back the drape, revealing the doctor attending the Queen. It was Elinor, unable to take her eyes off of Shakespeare. But he had not yet noticed her, so intent was he on diverting the Queen from her suffering.

"And thus they fought all the long day, and never stinted till the noble knights were laid to the cold earth; and ever they fought still till it was near night, and by that time was there an hundred thousand laid dead upon the down."

The Queen was following closely, and interrupted Shakespeare. "One wonders if it really could have been so many. What do you think, My Shakespeare?"

"I think the poet was using his license, Your Majesty. England was a smaller country then and unlikely could have massed so many."

"I think you are correct. Continue, if you would."

"Then was Arthur wood wroth out of measure, when he saw his people so slain from him."

Shakespeare at that moment happened to look away from the Queen and saw Elinor. He slowly absorbed the fact of her presence while he continued his recital.

" 'Now give me my spear,' said Arthur un Sir Lucan, 'for yonder I have espied the traitor that all this woe hath wrought.' 'Sir, let him be,' said Sir Lucan, 'For he is unhappy; and if ye pass this unhappy day ye shall be right well revenged upon him.'"

The Queen let out a gasp. "Doctor, this is causing me great distress. How much longer will you be?"

Elinor was soft and reassuring. "We are nearing the finish, Your Majesty. You are being quite brave."

The Queen put her head back into her pillow, but it was clear what she muttered next. "Don't treat me as a child."

Elinor again was reassuring. "Yes, Your Majesty."

Shakespeare continued, reading from the vast library in his memory.

"Then the king gat his spear in both his hands, and ran toward Sir Mordred, crying: Traitor, now is thy death-day come. And when Sir Mordred heard Sir Arthur, he ran until him with his sword drawn in his hand. And there King Arthur smote Sir Mordred under the shield, with a thrust of his spear, throughout the body, more than a fathom. And when Sir Mordred felt that he had his death wound he thrust himself with the might that he had up to the bur of King Arthur's spear.'"

Shakespeare looked at the Queen and saw that she had fallen asleep. He stood, looked up with his heart full of love for Elinor, and left the chamber.

Forty-Eight — For the Once and Future

*B*ackstage at the Globe, frenetic activity ruled as the crew worked up to the opening moments of the show. Jonathan Little was greenish-looking, obviously in the grip of a flu or worse. He was searching for someone, opening doors, pulling back drapes. Finally, he found Shakespeare holed up in a corner, copying out parts.

"Will?"

Shakespeare looked up and was alarmed. "Jonathan. You look the death."

"Scouts say your friend the Scottish king is in the house today. I cannot go on in this distress, and do it justice. Can you?"

Shakespeare was perplexed that James was there. "If he becomes King of England, the fate of theatre will be in his hands."

Little agreed. "Maybe we should change the play and put up something harmless, such as *Much Ado*."

Shakespeare disagreed. "He has come for the Danish play. He would resent our backing away."

Within the hour Shakespeare was on stage as Hamlet, at the moment dwarfed by a huge ghost that dominated the space, played by an actor draped in vast gauzes and lifted on stilts.

The ghost spoke. "…But know, thou noble youth, the serpent that did sting thy father's life now wears the crown."

Shakespeare as Hamlet let the terrible vision sink in. "O my prophetic soul! Mine uncle?"

Shakespeare's vision swept the crowd to gauge the impact of the ghost on them. He saw a familiar face in a box near the stage. Indeed, James, King of Scotland was there, trying to look unobtrusive. His gaze was on Shakespeare, and their glances met and held for a moment.

The ghost held the rest of the audience. "Ay, that incestuous, that adulterate beast. With witchcraft of his wit, with traitorous gifts."

James nodded in agreement with the mention of witchcraft, pleased that Shakespeare seemed to have used his research.

Shakespeare decided to make the point, and went off script. "Stay, Ghost?"

The ghost was genuinely startled. "Stay?"

"Did these ears hear of witchcraft?"

The ghost got the point. "Indeed! Witchcraft that seduced the will of my most seeming-virtuous queen."

By that point, the ghost was out of things to say, so Shakespeare brought the play back on track.

"Then, ghost, continue."

The play continued, and James remained enthralled. He felt as if the play had been written specifically to send him a coded message, and he watched it looking for revelations in every word.

As for Shakespeare's performance, he was making a justification for theatre directly to the man who might well hold its fate in his hand, if he were to become King.

Shakespeare was playing a Hamlet driven to find the truth. "The spirit that I have seen may be the devil: and the devil hath power to assume a pleasing shape; yea and perhaps out of my weakness and melancholy, as he is very potent with such spirits, abuses me to damn me: I'll have grounds."

Shakespeare then swept the audience from one edge to the other, having set it up so that he could land his gaze on King James. "More relative than this: the play's the thing wherein I'll catch the conscience of the king."

Hamlet ended to great applause, stamping of feet, and general cries for more. Shakespeare drew the actors on stage around him, and quieted the crowd.

He looked up at the open roof and gauged the light. "We have enough illumination for an encore. Would you like to hear from Richard the Second?"

There was a roar of approval and then the crowd settled down.

"For God's sake, let us sit upon the ground and tell sad stories of the death of kings; How some have been deposed; some slain in war, some haunted by the ghosts they have deposed."

King James was at the front of his box, and nodded his head with every Shakespearian insight.

"Some poison'd by their wives: some sleeping kill'd; All murder'd for within the hollow crown that rounds the mortal temples of a king keeps Death his court and there the antic sits, for you have but mistook me all this while: I live with bread like you, feel want, taste grief, need friends: subjected thus, how can you say to me, I am a king?"

In his box, James was deeply touched. Sensing his own mortality, he nodded in agreement with Shakespeare's Richard.

"All true, all true." He turned to an aide. "Have him brought here."

Forty-Nine — Divine Right has its Privileges

*T*he Globe was nearly empty. King James of Scotland held court in his box — with Lord Salisbury, Shakespeare, and various aides. There was food and drink, and candles were added again and again, making the box progressively brighter as the evening wore on.

King James enjoyed his theories. "I have come to understand you set your Hamlet in Denmark as a tribute to my young bride."

Shakespeare had not. But he was not about to correct the monarch. "My Lord, that would be so, in part. Partly also as a tribute to Denmark itself, and to those who had told the story there so many generations past."

James only partially understood, but felt complimented. "As I thought. Well done, well done. And have you read my thoughts on Divine Right?"

"I have read both of the treatises that I could find, the latest being The Trew Law of Free Monarchies."

"And your thoughts?"

Shakespeare hesitated, not untheatrically. "May I ask His Majesty a question regarding rhetoric first?"

The King allowed as how he was a great admirer of the rhetoric.

Shakespeare felt comfortable enough to venture forward. "Thank you, Your Majesty. Thus — if you were this poet," meaning himself, "and not yourself, and if you were completely and unalterably opposed to the notion that the authority of kings was an act of Divine providence, what might you say?"

Salisbury could not abide Shakespeare's impertinence with the King any longer.

"I would suggest the scoundrel be drawn and quartered."

James cut him off. "Thank you, Salisbury, but kindly hold your counsel." He turned back to Shakespeare. "Well put. I would hold my tongue or risk losing my theatre."

Shakespeare nodded, pleased. "And if I agreed with you?"

James was briefly puzzled, but worked it through. "I would say so."

Shakespeare now presented the king his perfectly prepared dish. "And how, then, would you know if you were speaking the truth?"

James was thrilled to be able to break Shakespeare's puzzle. "By the Divine right of my insight, of course! You may trust my divine insight to know whether you are speaking the truth, or merely to protect your interests."

Shakespeare positively gleamed. "So be it! In that case I must say I agree with both books."

James was delighted with both Shakespeare's wisdom and his own ability to know that the truth had just been spoken to him. "I knew it!"

Shakespeare ventured along. "And I have a further thought for your Majesty to consider."

"Salisbury, can you give us a moment?"

If Lord Salisbury was humiliated at being asked to leave, he was much too controlled to show it. With a dry smile, he bowed to the king and withdrew.

Shakespeare waited expectantly as James considered how best to say what he wanted to say.

"I need to thank you for something, but I am not clear exactly what the thing is I wish to express my gratitude for."

"Completely unnecessary, Your Majesty."

"No. Quite the opposite. It is completely necessary since it is so strange."

Shakespeare was even more intrigued. He said no more, and waited for the king to explain.

Finally, he spoke. "You have changed me."

Once more Shakespeare resisted the instinct to interject. He cocked his head a tiny bit just to show he had heard.

And then James continued. "When I first saw your people, the characters you put on the stage, when we met near Sheffield, wasn't it? And I saw your king and myself, and they were so different. And I have thought about that a great deal. Thought about it as I fall asleep. And when I ride."

Shakespeare listened, waiting.

"And I have been trying to understand that difference. Your king was not just a king — he was also a man, and knew that he was both. He knew that he was in the act of creating the king that he was. And I have begun to understand that I, too, if I am to be a great king, must also create that king."

Shakespeare nodded. As if to say thanks for what seemed to be a compliment, he managed to murmur, "Your Majesty."

"I did not know we had this power. And now I know that not only do I have it, but we all have this power, if only we know of it. Your plays show us that."

Shakespeare nodded.

Then King James cautioned him. "No one must ever know what I have told you."

"You have my eternal word. Rest assured."

"I accept. And now I have a favor to ask."

"There is nothing Your Highness might ask that if in my ability to perform, would be less than an honor."

James positively gleamed with excitement at what he was about to announce. "I have decided that the reforming of our Church would be better served if the general folk could read the scripture for themselves. I have gathered a broad committee from the clergy, scholars in the ancient languages, and all have been working to create our own English Bible."

Shakespeare had heard rumors, but that was all. "A magnificent enterprise. Visionary."

"I hope so. But it will only succeed if it also reflects the poetry of the Holy Word. I am afraid that we will fail if we rely on our many scholars and we end up with a hodge-podge of voices and styles and even words that are used differently here and there."

"That would be a shame, if it came to that."

"Therefore we need a final poetic voice that sees to all of it. That makes it one and whole."

King James looked at Shakespeare in the eye, as it dawned on Shakespeare what was about to be asked of him.

James read what he saw. "You look fearful."

"The favor?"

James gave him a wonderful smile. "I could simply command you."

Shakespeare did not protest. "I will do what I can. I hope you will not be disappointed."

James shook his head. "As we both know, I am guided by Divine wisdom. As you have recently concurred."

Fifty — The King's Man

King James and Lord Salisbury clattered along in the royal coach.

Salisbury was looking for a way to claw back some prestige. "Your Majesty, I look forward to the time when you have become King of England and we may be cleansed of these corrupting influences."

James seemed to agree at first, not paying too much attention. "I will do my best. Where might we begin?"

"Why, the theatre, Your Majesty. Its influence is already too great!"

King James imagined, for a moment, a world without theatre. Most of it gone wouldn't be that terrible. But a world without his Shakespeare? That was not comfortable.

He spoke with grave authority. "We will issue our warrants with great care, Salisbury. Mr. Shakespeare's group will become 'The King's Men,' and we'll look to the others from there."

"But…"

"That is the end of it."

Fifty-One — Shakespeare's Psalm

Will and Elinor were lying in bed. Neither knew it, but they were both wide awake, busy thinking. She rolled over, and then he did, fitting together as they always had.

He stated the obvious. "Are you sleeping?"

"No."

"Would you like to hear something? It is certain to make you drowsy."

"What is it?"

"What I have been working on."

"Do you need to light the lamp?"

"Hardly. It is running back and forth in my heart."

"Can't wait! Please begin."

Shakespeare took a moment to find the spot in his memory where he wanted to begin. "'This thy stature is like to a palm tree, and thy breasts to clusters of grapes.

"'I said, I will go up to the palm tree, I will take hold of the boughs thereof: now also thy breasts shall be as clusters of the vine, and the smell of thy nose like apples;

"'And the roof of thy mouth like the best wine for my beloved, that goeth down sweetly, causing the lips of those that are asleep to speak.'"

Elinor interrupted. "I doubt that the roof of my mouth is like that."

"You'd be wrong."

Shakespeare continued, "I think you'll like this part. 'I am my beloved's, and his desire is toward me. Come, my beloved, let us go forth into the field; let us lodge in the villages.

"Let us get up early to the vineyards; let us see if the vine flourish, whether the tender grape appear, and the pomegranates bud forth: there will I give thee my loves.'"

Elinor was both delighted and puzzled. "Quite lovely, and yet, this seems so familiar. Is this another Venus and Adonis?"

"Would that it were. This is from the Song of Solomon. I had saved it for last."

Each eventually fell into a deep sleep, and when the dawn came they were reluctant to get out of bed.

Shakespeare saw where the sunlight was streaking across the shutters, and was suddenly wide awake. "I will have a coach waiting in a moment. We must get up!"

• ⋅⋅ ⦃•❍❂❍•⦄⋗⋅⋅ •

The following morning, when he arrived at the Merton Library at Oxford, a dozen scholars were already at work.

He settled at his desk overlooked by a semi-circle of ancient leaded glass windows.

An elderly, dusty clerk soon arrived with a stack of loose sheets.

"Good morning, sir. Here we have the last of the psalms."

"Rexford, are these actually the very last psalms that will fall to me?"

"Regretfully, sir, they are."

"Our date for publication is still the eleventh year of this century, correct?"

"That is our plan, sir."

Shakespeare noodled on a piece of scrap vellum, working out some numbers.

Shakespeare looked up at Rexford. "Is the forty-sixth somewhere?"

Rexford knew where everything was and soon produced it.

Shakespeare examined the manuscript. It said 'Forty-Six' on the top, followed by 'For the leader. Of the Korahites; on alamoth.' The word alamoth was circled.

Shakespeare looked around for his clerk, who had slipped away. "Reference!"

The clerk magically reappeared. "Sir?"

"Rexford, have we tracked down the meaning of alamoth yet?"

"It is Hebrew, sir, and so obscure that none of our books have it. I have also asked 'round and so far, we have nothing."

Shakespeare was perplexed for the moment. "Then let it stand for this edition."

Shakespeare dipped his quill and wrote 'stet' next to alamoth.

He looked at the working text of Psalm Forty-Six and came across the line, 'its waters rage and foam; in its swell mountains quake.'

Shakespeare quietly said to himself, "If they can quake, they can certainly shake."

He struck out the 'quake' and made his substitution. And then he counted the word from the beginning of the psalm.

"Forty-two. 'In its swell the mountains shake.'" He puzzled for a moment. "Why not 'mountains shake with the swelling thereof?'"

Shakespeare looked up from his labors and called out. "Reference!"

Rexford soon appeared. "Sir?"

Shakespeare gave him a level eye. "Rexford, are you capable of keeping a trust?"

Rexford read the twinkle in Shakespeare's eye. "I serve but one master, sir. In this library and your efforts, it is you."

"Excellent. Listen to how this section plays its meter: 'Though the waters thereof roar and be troubled, though the mountains shake with the swelling thereof.'

Rexford paused appropriately. "It lands quite musically upon the ear, I would think."

Shakespeare gave him a conspiratorial glance. "And would it surprise you that in the year 1611, when, if the Lord shall so grant, I will be forty-six years old? And here, in Psalm Forty-Six, should one count from the first word, they might notice that word forty-six is 'shake.' Do you think anyone would notice or be bothered?"

Rexford was puzzled. "Shake, sir? Seems harmless enough. What is the issue?"

Shakespeare gave him the clue. "It is, in fact, the first part of my family name. Wouldn't that jolt the reader?"

Rexford shook his head in the negative. "I very much doubt that anyone would. Ever. Few know of your involvement as it is. And further, sir, if I may, without all of your name present, who would ever divine it was a signature?"

"Maybe you are right. Perhaps I am being overly obscure. I will need to count from the end and see if I can embed the rest of the puzzle."

Rexford was delighted at the secret. "I wish you well in your subterfuge, Sir."

Fifty-Two — Small Things Made Large

*S*hades of a domestic life had descended upon Elinor and Shakespeare in London. At the moment, they were enjoying a private, celebratory dinner, with servants quietly in the background.

Will raised his glass. "Here we are on the final day of the third year in this new century. A toast to our Queen." He sipped from his glass, and then added, "May she survive her doctor's ministrations…"

Elinor laughed with him. "She's tougher than I had first thought."

"In fact, she would not be amongst the living without you."

"Thank you."

Shakespeare offered another toast. "To the Queen, who has given England a vibrant theatre not known since that of the ancient Greeks."

Elinor agreed with a clink. "To The Queen."

"And a toast to our present Scottish king and future King of England. May he enjoy a reign of tranquility."

Elinor agreed. "To James Six and James One."

Shakespeare was momentarily confused by the numbering. "Is that correct?"

Elinor explained what she had heard in the palace. "I believe he will change his digit from his Scottish number six to a British designation of one"

"How curious. To Six and to One."

They toasted again, and then Elinor called for a servant, who brought some boxes.

Elinor simply said, "For you."

Shakespeare took the topmost of the elaborately wrapped boxes, and carefully opened it. He dug in the contents for a moment, and then understood. "Ah! Sand! To blot out the wicked mistakes and dry the blood the effort makes."

He played with the blotting sand for a moment, being silly. "Take thee to an island!"

Elinor was serene. "Open more."

Will took the second box and brought out the treasure. "What have we? The finest ink from India. Indelible."

"Now I hope you'll write something worth keeping."

Will nodded with great seriousness. "I will so endeavor. Now."

He opened the third box, and produced a beautiful gold nib and an outrageous feathered quill. "Oh, this is splendid. No more excuses. Thank you, my darling. Marvelous way to start the century. And now, yours."

He nodded to his servant waiting nearby, who brought in a good-sized rough wooden case, which he set on a table and drew it close to Elinor. The servant helped her with the final fasteners.

Elinor appraised the rugged shipping container. "Something romantic, I can tell."

Shakespeare nodded. "Extremely."

From the box, with some help, she withdrew a microscope, all brass tubes, stages and lenses.

Elinor could barely contain her excitement. "Is this what I think it is?"

Shakespeare nodded. "The rumors are true. A Dutchman has made a device for seeing the invisible. This is the first in England."

Elinor got up from the table and came back with something folded in a tiny piece of paper. She fitted it on a glass and slid it into the microscope. After fiddling, and drawing many candles close, she turned a dial and suddenly saw something.

"A flea I have been saving for just such an occasion. I have always wanted to see one better."

Shakespeare peered into the microscope. "Ah! There it is! I can see something. A tiny monster!"

He looked up from the microscope to look at Elinor. They were very, very happy for the moment.

Shakespeare held her at arm's length and gazed at her shining beauty. "Our world holds such endless wonders."